HARD MAN TO KILL

Dark Horse Guardians: Book 4

Sequel to Flawlessly Executed

Written by

Ava Armstrong

A dark horse is a little-known person or thing

that emerges to prominence,

especially in a competition of some sort

or a contestant

that seems unlikely to succeed.

TABLE OF CONTENTS

Prologue

~Abdul Rahman Shafir~

Abdul waited patiently for hours in the darkness, crouched in the tall weeds just south of the river. The figure he had been tracking for days stepped out of the safe house, into the darkness on the outskirts of the city of Khost.

Sweating profusely and shaking, Abdul raised the night vision goggles and focused on the silhouette. Abdul was not certain if the imposing outline was that of Lieutenant Ben Keegan, but he had orders to follow this man if he emerged.

The first question that ran through his mind was: *exactly how do you follow an assassin who stalks his prey for a living? First, don't let him see you.*

Abdul's dark skin and black clothing concealed him in the shadows as he tracked the man along the riverbank, barely moving. Abdul's target faced the river and waved his arm once. Abdul observed a boat as it glided soundlessly toward him. The man leapt upon the boat as if he'd done it a thousand times, with athletic precision. The boat moved slowly down the Indus River and out of sight, but he knew it was heading south. Abdul sent a text to Ibrahim giving him the coordinates of the vessel.

If it was Keegan, Abdul knew this man had been to Pakistan many times, was familiar with the terrain, and had hundreds of contacts. And, it was entirely possible, that if it was Keegan, he knew he was being followed. For three years Abdul heard stories about this ghost, trained as an American Navy SEAL. They said he was unstoppable, but "they" gossiped like women. Abdul and Ibrahim had found a way to stop him. It would not be easy, but anything magnificent never really was. His father had taught him that.

Abdul hoped he would be the one chosen to slit Keegan's throat. He was silently thanking Allah for the recent Senate Intelligence Report. Because he could read English proficiently, Abdul had the massive document plopped on his desk by his superior a month earlier. Although only eyes and mouth were visible in the delivery man's head wrap, Abdul knew the report was sent by his father from a Muslim Fellowship friend in the State Department. This task was of utmost importance, and could propel him to the highest levels of the Islamic state.

"Find this Keegan," Salib Madi, his father, spat angrily as he spoke when he met him after finishing with the document. The frustration with Keegan had reached a crescendo. The former Navy SEAL had easily killed over a hundred of their men. And, those were only the ones they knew about. Abdul poured over the American intelligence report and found the name of an informant, Nazmin, a woman in Pakistan. When he brought the information to his father, he was so pleased, Madi allowed Abdul to assist in planning the raid of her home. Abdul helped more experienced fighters decapitate her, then placed her head upon a spit for the rest of the village to see. He worked with the men to kill all of the women and children on her property. He destroyed the safe house the Americans had been lurking in, plotting and planning against his holy jihad. He played the YouTube video over and over. It was his first.

Abdul spoke in Arabic as they filmed him. "This public act of decapitation serves as a message to the world: this is what happens when you help these American pigs. This will be your fate, unless you submit to Islamic reign." But the savage acts did not satisfy his father. Salib Madi now wanted the ultimate revenge. Keegan.

Abdul knew that, eventually, one of Madi's men would capture this Keegan. But he wanted the honor of slitting his throat. His half-brother, Ibrahim, was more interested in the bounty. Either way, Keegan was a walking dead man. They had dedicated their lives to follow him to the ends of the earth if necessary. From what he read in the intelligence report, it might just be necessary.

One more piece of information gleaned from the report was where Keegan lived in the United States. He taught at a well-known university and lived in a beautiful home on the Atlantic Ocean. This information was buried in the document, but Abdul discovered it and decided to act on his own. He wanted nothing more than to rise to the top. He could only do so if he demonstrated leadership and dedication. Tapping his laptop out of sleep-mode, he sent a tweet to two men already in the United States, waiting for an assignment. Abdul gave them the address and description of Lara Keegan.

End Prologue

Chapter 1

~ Ben ~

Early morning was his favorite time to make love. He heard Lara in the bathroom washing her hands and face and knew her habit was to brush her teeth upon rising. But it was too early for her to rise for the day. It was only 4:00. He felt her slip back underneath the sheet and waited as she tugged the heavy blanket over her. He listened as she exhaled and relaxed before rolling toward her. Snuggling up to her backside, he tucked his arm over the curve of her waist so he could pull her to him if she tried to move away.

He knew Lara loved it when he nestled his body closely behind her like this. She wanted his body heat, but more than that, she loved his touch. Inhaling the scent of her thick dark hair at the nape of her neck excited him. His erection touched the soft skin of her shapely rear, and as it grew, so did the urgency inside of him. The effect she had on him was automatic whenever he was awake, and sometimes when he was asleep. His body flooded with hormones and within seconds he was ready for anything she might want.

Within a minute she turned to face him, hair askew, lips slightly parted, eyes half-closed. He thought he'd died and gone to heaven. His mouth covered hers, as he moved slightly above her kissing those soft full lips that he craved every minute of every day.

She was naked and his hand reached around and pulled her firm bottom toward him.

"Damn, I want you..." he whispered into the crook of her neck, defeated by her feminine powers long ago. Lara giggled and ran her hands through his hair, then he felt one hand behind his head pulling his mouth to hers. Her other hand touched his and guided it slowly between her legs. A shot of adrenaline went through him like a bolt of lightning. This is what he wanted more than anything in the world. The velvet warmth of her kiss shot spirals of ecstasy through him. Touching the wetness between her legs nearly drove him crazy. Raising his mouth from hers, he gazed into Lara's eyes. As his hand moved, he felt gusts of desire moving through her and watched with fascination as she climaxed.

Breathing erratically, Lara whispered, "Oh, Ben, I love you."

She was now a heady image of fire, passion and love in the dimly lit room. He belonged to her. When she touched him, he ached with desire. She sensed his arousal and stroked him tenderly.

"Yes," she whispered over and over.

After only a few minutes, his need for her grew desperate, frenzied. His hard body moved atop hers, and they linked in a way that was instinctive. Her body arched upward meeting his. He gazed into her eyes with every stroke, and she matched his urgency with her own yearning, wrapping her arms and legs around him, trapping him against her. Pure pleasure moved through him, building, mounting to the ultimate peak of arousal. He heard her whimpering and knew she was hitting the peak of desire. Simultaneously, the hot tide of passion ran through both of them as he groaned and she ~~sighed~~whimpered.

"Shh—" Lara placed her finger on his lips. "You'll wake William!"

Moments later he held her in his arms, "I love you, Lara, more than you can ever imagine."

"I love you, Ben," she sighed. He could feel her heart beating wildly.

"Happy, darlin?" he whispered.

"Completely, when I'm with you." She tucked her head under his chin and ran her hand over his chest. He loved it when she touched his chest. She knew exactly what he liked, every little detail. He inhaled deeply observing her, wanting to hold this image in his memory forever. He would need the image of this perfect moment to keep as a luscious dream cradled in the back of his mind, as he knew he had a long, hard trek ahead of him.

Thinking back on the past few days, Ben felt he had solidified a bond with his son and with Lara that was resilient. At least he got to spend *one* Christmas Day at home and discovered the joys of putting up a Christmas tree with his son. Lieutenant Ben Keegan hadn't known that pleasure since, well, since he could remember. The last time he had a so-called normal Christmas was in the Naval Academy, before he had married his first wife, before William was born. For the last twelve years, Christmas was just another working day. As a Navy SEAL in theater, he'd be lucky to get a piece of turkey in the green zone; if he was on work-ups between tours, sometimes he could get back to see his parents. However, those visits were few and far between, not only because they were difficult to synchronize, but because it was emotional to come home for one or two days. Leaving was heart-breaking, especially when you were unable to discuss what you were doing.

But this Christmas was different. Today, as he held Lara in his arms, he would carry the pleasant remembrance of this one special Christmas in his pocket, like a touchstone, to pull out once in a while to turn over. It meant so much to him to connect with William. Their relationship was different than the typical father-son, but in some ways much deeper. He vowed after this upcoming mission, he would see more of his son, bring him to Maine in the summer months to go sailing and to vacation at the cottage on Prince Edward Island. It was a vow that he had always made to himself in the past, but a vow that had never stayed intact. Until now. He was certain of it this time.

Once Moshe contacted Ben about the Guantanamo hunting expedition, the clock in his head started ticking. There was a deadline, and all of his team members were more than happy to participate in the mission. It was as if Ben had invited them to the biggest, badass New Year's Eve party on the planet. But his men were the type would who take on the Terminator for a six-pack and the promise of a good time. With the addition of Randall Bettencourt to the group, the dynamic would be different. Bettencourt having been a SEAL himself, and a law enforcement officer, gave him a skillset that encompassed multiple disciplines. More importantly, Ben loved and trusted the man. Respect was everything in this profession and Bettencourt had earned it exponentially.

It had been difficult to say goodbye to William so abruptly, but even more so to Lara. The look in her hazel-green eyes said everything he needed to know. She became reticent, hardened, and he knew she would be crying later. But she kissed him with passion and the taste of her lingered. Her kiss, her dedication to his cause, her love would sustain him while away. She probably had no idea how much having her to come back to meant to him. He couldn't put it into words. But he planned to show her when he returned. She joked he was her favorite hello. She was his everything.

Some folks viewing their relationship from the outside might think they were too dependent upon one another. But, from his perspective he knew he'd found his soulmate, as corny as that might sound. Ben felt Lara not only completed him, but that they completed each other. They could barely stand to be apart from each other for more than a day, let alone weeks or months.

As he sped toward Logan airport in his wreck of a rental vehicle, he thought about Lara and struggled with the guilty feeling of leaving her again so soon. But she got it. When an opportunity like this came up, he had to take it. She was the rare woman who understood that this was his calling. His pulse quickened as he spoke on the Bluetooth to check-in with each team member.

In record time, he parked his battered Nissan in the long-term garage. He met the team members on the shuttle that took them to the C-130J Hercules waiting on the tarmac at Logan, silently thanking Moshe. The men tossed their gear on the ground and an attendant pulled it all inside the plane. There was no time to waste. The smell of the tarmac, jet fuel and freshly washed laundry was familiar as he boarded. As soon as the pilot found a pocket of free airspace, they were wheels up heading for Hatzor Airbase in Israel. From there they would meld with The Sayeret Matkal Unit for a week-long run-through in a mock-up of the area of operations. The team would train around the clock, utilizing the Dark Horse war gaming software. Ahead were long days and nights putting together the puzzle of intel they had garnered from human intelligence on the ground.

Once in flight, the chatter died down. As the engines roared at cruising altitude, Ben curled himself into a fetal position and fell asleep. As he closed his eyes, he imagined the thrill it would be to kill the bastards they had incarcerated in the comfortable country club confines of Guantanamo Bay, Cuba. These sons-of-bitches had superior medical care and a better lifestyle than the veterans who were arriving home from Afghanistan and Iraq. Nothing made him angrier than the way the American government pampered these war criminals at Guantanamo.

Nothing would give him more satisfaction to put them away –
permanently.

What pissed him off even more was according to the Geneva
Convention, America was well within their rights to take each and every
"illegal combatant," put two bullets in their heads, and dump them *into*
the bay around Guantanamo. But the liberals and the press were
demanding, insisting, shouting, screaming – and the White House was
giving in.

Ben could barely stop the smile that spread across his face as he
lie in the belly of the C-130J Hercules. They'd be hunting men who had
been living a lavish lifestyle, fatted calves. They'd be easy to pick off.
Maybe it was a good thing these bastard jihadists had been sunning
themselves, eating their favorite foods, lazy and out of the fight for so
long. They had time to grow slow and complacent. It would be akin to a
wolf hunting a domesticated dog.

Knowing they were being released, the terrorists probably felt
safe. They'd want to celebrate with friends and loved ones and, most
likely, that's where they'd make first contact. Ben had been in touch with
Moshe only twice since accepting the mission, but he knew the men they
were hunting were being tracked with round-the-clock vigilance and the
plan was being formulated in his battle-hardened mind. This was the
mission he had been waiting for. He slept soundly even though a tinge of
excitement ran through his veins. This sleep was like the night before
Christmas.

*It was the night after Christmas, and all through the plan, not a
jihadi was stirring, not one single man. The weapons were stored in their
holsters with care, in the hopes that a firefight soon would be there.* Ben
fell asleep with a smile.

~ Lara ~

Most women would be crying. Lara would save that for when Ben returned, *if* he returned. Every time he left, she felt if she was holding her breath. Christmas had been so beautiful with Ben there, sharing the moments with William. She was preparing to drive William to the airport tomorrow. She packed Ben's Navy SEAL trident carefully and shipped it special delivery to Will's address in Canada. Most likely the TSA would confiscate an object like that as Will passed through security at the airport, and she knew it would break his heart.

William seemed unaffected by Ben's abrupt departure. *Resilience.* It was something that she imagined had been passed down genetically to William from Ben, a spirit of acceptance and determination to forge ahead. This would be Will's last night at Clearwater Farm and she wanted it to be special for her step-son.

Lara glanced at William. "Hey, I'm making some cocoa. Do you want some?"

"Sure. Can I have marshmallows in mine?" William smiled.

"Of course. Do you want to watch a movie tonight?"

"I wanted to play *A Sense of Duty*, you know, my computer game. Would you like to play, too?" "My friends will be on in an hour."

She was surprised he invited her into his private domain with his closest school chums.

"Yes, I'd like to *try* it, at least. I might not be very good." Lara chuckled.

"No, you'd be great." William sounded sure of himself. "Dad said you shoot guns at the range and you're a good shot."

Lara rolled her eyes. "Really, he said that?" *I wonder how often they talk about me. Huh.*

The two of them drank cocoa and watched *America's Funniest Videos*, something that she often watched with Ben. Their belly-laughs filled the living room for an hour.

William turned to her. "Meet me upstairs in my bedroom. It's time. My friends will all be on-line to play A Sense of Duty."

"Okay," Lara answered as she cleaned up the kitchen. She never imagined she'd be playing a war game with a ten-year old on Christmas night, but she wanted to sneak a peek into William's world. His bedroom was dimly lit when she entered, and he handed her a headset with built-in goggles. William was in his pajamas and speaking into a small microphone.

"OK, guys. This is my step-mother, Lara. She might surprise you." William spoke with certainty. Lara was amazed that he thought so highly of her skills. She suddenly hoped she would not disappoint him.

Once she slipped the 3D goggles on, the game began in earnest with her being introduced as Slapshot. She got a quick tour of the controller and began to select her weaponry. The realism of the game was mind-boggling. As she went through the most basic kill scenes, she imagined this was exactly what Ben encountered in *real combat* during his tours in Iraq and Afghanistan. How anyone could do this for a more than a decade was beyond her comprehension.

Meanwhile, William was talking to his friends who all had nicknames, like Blade and Juice, and a few others she didn't want to acknowledge. They were instantly planning the strategy and tactics of a mission, and the game had many directions in which it could go. After two hours of explosions, rifle blasts, grenades being launched, and futuristic weaponry, Lara tapped out. Her character had been killed five times before she even figured out how to maneuver the controller.

William nodded to her as she left his room, but he was teeing up for a battle level far beyond what she had just experienced. As she padded barefoot back down to the living room, she sat by the woodstove and gazed out at the ocean, wondering where Ben was at that very moment. He was airborne, that much she knew. And, just through being observant she knew this mission was huge. She knew everything Ben did was top secret, but this time she had a sinking feeling he may have taken on more than he could handle.

Her phone vibrated and she jumped nervously. It was Monique, Bett's girlfriend. Lara listened to her halting words. It was obvious she had been crying and was at the end of a lengthy jag. Lara spoke softly into the phone and simply said, "Now you know the feeling."

With her voice quivering, Monique ranted, "He just slipped a beautiful engagement ring on my finger. I was so happy. Now, the man of my dreams is off on the other side of the world. I don't even know *where* he is. I don't know if I'll ever see him again."

Lara could tell she had lost all semblance of self-control. She was raw, terrified, and panic-stricken.

"Why don't you come over tonight? You shouldn't be alone. It is Christmas, after all. I'm here with William. Stay here tonight."

Monique took her up on the offer. She had just spent the day at her parents' home nearby. Lara sensed she needed to unload her pent up frustration. Her mother and step-father, Rusty, would be stopping by in the morning for pancakes to say goodbye to William. Maybe Monique would enjoy that diversion, even if for a few hours.

Little did Monique know how much her companionship would be welcomed, especially once William departed for Canada. Except for Einstein, the house would be empty. It would be a joy to have someone to keep her company. The dog was a wonderful comfort, but Lara was fighting the same feelings of fear, and lived with a sick feeling in the pit of her stomach until Ben returned unharmed. Until then, she would put on a good front -- but when alone she'd crumble into a heap of tears at the slightest provocation.

Chapter 2

Israel

~ Ben ~

Arrival at Hatzor airbase was routine for the team. Moshe's men met them and helped to carry and load their gear into an armored vehicle. Not even Ben knew how many men Moshe commanded. It was a closely guarded secret and the forces were constantly shifting and modernizing to meet new demands. Every Israeli citizen served in the military, and Israel's Institute for Intelligence reserved the right to call upon the service of any Jew on the planet.

The United States could learn a great deal from this tiny nation with an innate instinct to survive.

Institute for Intelligence was simply known as "the Institute," or simply "Mossad." Mossad was the executive branch of the counter-terrorism unit, but it operated differently than the Central Intelligence Agency in America. There were off-shoots specifically trained and designated to perform intelligence tasks. These groups could turn on a dime. Their nimble readiness and high level of training was a thing of beauty. He felt fortunate to be this close to some of the greatest warriors in the world.

The war room was a short drive away and the Dark Horse Guardians got into the armored vehicles for transport to the place where they'd live for the next few days.

"Was the flight comfortable?" Moshe slapped Ben on the back. "It should have been. We just purchased a boatload of these J's from the United States. They're beautiful."

Moshe was an aerodynamic junkie. He loved anything that had an engine and wings. Having been trained as a pilot in his earlier years, he was intimately familiar with every plane in the fleet. He should be; he ordered them.

"Yes," Ben responded sleepily. "So comfortable, I slept for five hours. A big upgrade, I'd say. They know how to make them in Atlanta. Quality workmanship."

Ben rode in Moshe's private SUV, with enough armor to survive a nuclear attack. Inside the vehicle was a dashboard with a unique com system. Moshe lived with an earpiece and tiny microphone twenty-four hours a day. Ben imagined he made love to Rachel with it on. As the drive took them toward their destination, Moshe's dark black eyes looked into Ben's.

"You ready for this?" he mused. "I'm jacked."

"You've had one too many espressos," Ben joked with him. But then he became deadly serious. "Yes, I'm ready. I've been waiting to beat these guys to death with my bare hands ever since I heard of the first ones being released back onto the battlefield. After watching on YouTube what these jihadist-bastards have done, the heinous crimes against humanity – I don't need any more inspiration. And, I think I just might sucker punch the next idiot who bitches about how awful it is to water board them."

Moshe smiled. "Ah, you're ready. I have the records waiting in the war room."

"The more information we have, the better. We need it all, their habits, what they eat. You got the data from Gitmo, right?" Ben queried.

"Yes, and we even have footage of their activities while there. It's very telling. We will watch some of that in the war room."

Ben nodded. Rule number one, *know thine enemy*. Moshe would occasionally joke that rule number two was, *kill them wherever you find them*. Ben knew the verse was from the Quran, referring to Muslims being instructed to kill infidels. But, now this theory was turned upon the jihadists. Fighting fire with fire was Moshe's strategy, and it was working.

The team scrambled to the plain white building, entered, and walked down a flight of stairs leading to a tunnel. Fifty feet beneath the ground was a steel-reinforced bunker the size of a city-block. Personnel of all stripes were gathering data, preparing for the briefing in the war room. The Dark Horse Guardians were led to their sleeping quarters. Moshe put his hand on Ben's shoulder.

"We're in this together." He said with a defiant little smirk.

"Damn straight." Ben smiled back. "Let's do this."

~ Lara ~

It was a good idea she asked Monique to spend the night. Her friend was exhausted from crying and worrying about Bettencourt on his first Dark Horse mission. Lara could only comfort her and listen. She was all too familiar with the fear and uncertainty. She knew it would be best to let Monique rant and rave for a while. She had to get it out of her system before she could speak sensibly.

At one in the morning, after two hours of listening to her ride the roller coaster of emotions, Lara said, "You've got to eat something, Monique. "You'll just feel worse if you don't."

"Okay," Monique acquiesced, "Maybe something."

"Scrambled eggs and toast?" Lara offered.

Monique curled up on the sofa. Lara tossed her a blanket and switched the television on, finding a crazy late night show. Eventually Monique showed signs of watching it. Once she saw Monique smile, Lara allowed herself to laugh at some of the outrageous comments. Then Lara noticed Monique was shoveling scrambled eggs into her mouth.

Good, the distraction was working. After a night of sleep, Monique would begin to stabilize. Her spirit would start the process of strengthening. It was a sort of self-preservation that would take place one day at a time. But the waxing and waning was the difficult part. The reinforcement of one's soul did not take place overnight.

By 2:00 AM they were tucked into bed. Monique in the guest room and Lara in the big empty bed she shared with Ben. His sandalwood scent lingered in the sheets and she would not change the bed until he returned. It as a ritual, a crazy superstition. She slept on his side, inhaling his masculine smell and wept silently before falling asleep. She prayed to God to keep him safe, but knew the evil forces Ben was fighting were strong and doing all that they could to blot out anything to do with God or goodness.

In the morning, Lara made pancakes for her mother, Rusty, Monique, and an extra-large serving for William. Driving William to the airport and saying goodbye was painful. But his face exuded happiness, and that was all that mattered at the moment. With a tear in her eye, she watched as William boarded the plane and it was cleared for take-off. She stood in front of the plate glass window at the Portland Airport wondering if he could see her waving.

Once William's plane was airborne, she turned and embraced Monique. The two held one another as if they'd just been through their own internal war, holding back their real feelings, not allowing weakness or sorrow to register. Lara rubbed Monique on the back.

"We're good. You know what we need to do right now?" Lara asked.

"What…" Monique asked with a bit of hesitation.

"We need to go to the spa and soak in a hot tub and get a massage." Lara suggested.

"Are they open today?"

"Yes, I made the appointment last week, knowing I'd probably need it after Christmas. I'll make sure there's a massage therapist available for you." Lara tapped her Bluetooth and spoke to the spa receptionist. "There you go. There was a cancellation this morning. You get a massage, and I'm paying." Lara smiled as they got into the Mercedes.

"I've never had one before." Monique confessed.

"Well, let me tell you this: once you get a massage, you'll be hooked." Lara giggled.

"I don't have a swim suit with me." Monique said.

"Don't need one. They have disposable ones there," Lara informed her. "It's just the two of us in a huge tub of swirling 103 degree water. Not to worry."

Lara thought she saw the beginning of a smile on Monique's face. Good. She at least was thinking of something *else* for a few minutes instead of whatever horrible scenario her new fiancé might be experiencing.

As the Mercedes pulled up to the spa, the two jumped out and traced a path through the freshly fallen snow. Just what both women needed, a bit of pampering and a chance to talk about hair and make-up and clothing...ordinary things, really, but fun nonetheless.

The door to the spa stuck. As Lara attempted to close it, she caught a glimpse of a blacked out Mustang from the corner of her eye. The car whizzed by and didn't stop.

How many Mustangs are there in this neck of the woods? Because I could have sworn I saw that one at the airport. There was a brief moment of paranoia, but she remembered that, usually, undercover law enforcement guys drove blacked out Mustangs. The thought flitted through her mind momentarily that Bettencourt knew many of the local law men in the area. It was possible that he'd asked one of the detectives to keep an eye on her while he was away. That would be so like him.

As they head for the spa reception area, Lara reached for her phone.

"Who are you calling?" Monique quizzed her.

"Bettencourt."

Monique's face became serious. "Why?"

Before Lara could answer, the familiar voice boomed over the speaker, "Bettencourt."

"Hey, you – I have a question. Did you put a tail on us for safe keeping while you're gone?" Lara asked. There was a long pause on the line. "Are you there?"

"I heard you," Bettencourt said haltingly, "Let me check with Ben." She heard Ben's voice muffled in the background. "No. We didn't. What does the vehicle look like?"

"It's a blacked-out Mustang, brand new. You know, the type the undercover guys use." Lara explained. She felt a chill run through her.

"Listen, Lara. Be careful. Someone might be following you, but I don't know who the hell it is. Take precautions. See a guy named Paul Simpson at the station. Give him the description and license plate and details…mention my name. But, for God's sake, watch your back. We're taking off. I have to go…." And the phone went dead.

Israel

~ Ben ~

In the war room, Moshe gave his presentation on the targets. Ben had already read the intel reports on the Gitmo detainees and knew full well what their crimes were. The list went on for a while. It was long, horrific, and read like a valid argument for an official war to be declared on the jihadist bastards who called themselves the Islamic State. The victims' photos were on full high-definition display in front of the men to help them wrap their heads around the level of evil these men had perpetrated. The screen was the size of a movie theater's, and as the photos accumulated, they had to be shrunk to thumbnail size, just to fit them all on the screen. To describe these as crimes against humanity would be an understatement. Between the mass rapes, mass graves, and wrought-iron fences with decapitated heads on *every single spike*, this rivaled, and perhaps surpassed, the tyranny of the Nazi regime.

Fierce determination flooded through Ben. This was a job that had to be done, nothing more. Although, he hated these creatures who looked like men, he would not let emotion rule. He temporarily suspended his ability to feel as he got into the mission. He became cold and hollow, emptied of everything but the focus on what lie ahead. He was conscious of this necessary transformation. As his eyes glanced around the room, he noticed every one of his men were going through that very same process as they listened to Moshe's detailed report. He watched as their eyes soaked in photo after photo. There was a palpable silence as he sensed their mental state harden.

Afterward, they filed to the dining hall and ate. There were a few hours of reading to do for mission prep. The men retired to their separate chambers to absorb detailed material regarding the mission. Ben took a moment, tapped his phone and glanced at the security system at Clearwater Farm. The house was empty. Einstein was asleep in his dog bed in the kitchen. He knew that his son was home in Canada by now. Ben scrolled through the photographs of William on his phone that he'd taken Christmas Eve. His son was turning into a man. He thought of calling him, but he was several time zones away. William would be sleeping. Instead, he sent him a text, *Hi, it's Dad. Thinking of you. Glad we got to be together for Christmas. Love you.*

He couldn't even think of Lara. He would be too strongly tempted to get on the first plane back home. Ben flopped onto his bunk in private quarters and turned on a small reading light. He read for an hour, memorizing every detail. Mock-ups and work-ups were always the most important segment of the mission plan. The Dark Horse game was equally as important, as it presented elements of danger the men hadn't considered during their practice sessions. Tonight they'd utilize the high-tech software to go through each scenario with enhanced satellite images and chats with human intelligence on the ground. *Updates.* They always changed everything slightly, sometimes for the better.

But something was gnawing at him. The hyper-vigilance kicked in, as it often did during mission prep. Restless, Ben grabbed Moshe out of the war room long enough to check the storage locker.

"I've already done this, bro." Moshe smiled. "But we can double-check. I know how you like to do that, just a little bit obsessive-compulsive."

Ben smiled. "Rule number 3, it's not obsessive-compulsion if it works."

For the next hour Moshe and Ben went over every pistol, long gun, magazine, laser sight, night-vision equipment, body armor, black face masks and disguises, right down to the cigarettes they'd smoke. And, as Ben suspected, they were short on a few items. Sunglasses, for example. They needed a specific style, and Ben decided on more hypodermic needles, extras just in case one failed.

Once he exhausted the list and the additional items were packed, he felt he could relax just a little before the Dark Horse computer simulation began. He closed his eyes on the bunk for fifteen minutes to take a short nap. Too short.

Elvis woke him. "Hey Chief, let's go."

In the Dark Horse simulation, Ben's team assembled with Moshe's unit and they got down to business. Since September 11th, 775 detainees had been brought to Guantanamo Bay, Cuba. Although most of those captured were released without formal charges, the American government continued to classify many released as enemy combatants, a nice phrase for bonafide terrorists. As of December 2014, 132 detainees remained at Guantanamo. Over 600 had been released, and their whereabouts were the subject of discussion. Many of these men were living in banana republics, such as Venezuela, Ecuador, Guatemala and Columbia. Some were back in Afghanistan, Yemen, Pakistan and Syria now running the Islamic uprising that the Commander-in-Chief refused to call Islamic. Some had been put into the ground by Ben and his men.

And, there was a new twist. Thanks to a group of disgruntled liberals on the Senate Intelligence Committee with a grudge against the current CIA Director, information was about to be systematically leaked to the press. Ben compared this betrayal to the rat bastard that worked for the NSA and fled to Russia. The leaking of classified information was earth-shattering to special ops and human intelligence assets on the ground, doing their jobs day and night -- risking their lives.

It was only a matter of time before the terrorists who were released would be informed of their impending demise. But the kill order had been given with a narrow window of opportunity specified. Thus, time was critical for this mission to succeed. There was plenty of killing to do, but it had to be done swiftly and with great precision.

Coordinates for the first hit were set up on the enormous screens before them. Ben dreaded working in the banana republic even more than Afghanistan. There would be Malaria to contend with along with Dengue and Yellow Fever, and Chagas. These parasitic diseases were common for workers in the forests of South America. He hoped the recent shipment to Moshe's storage facility of protective combat undergarments would help protect the men, but it was no guarantee.

Besides the bugs there were leeches and water snakes. Crocodiles the size of stretch hummers, rats and wild boars added interest to the jungle adventure, along with a long list of predators in the animal kingdom who would be stalking him. Guatemala was a hell hole. He never thought he'd prefer the terrain of Afghanistan and Iraq to anything, but the race to the bottom was won by Latin America for fighting hand-to-hand combat in piss-poor conditions.

Four hours passed with details, movements, friendlies, safe houses, everything carefully and methodically marked so that each hit would be perfect. Of most concern, the algorithms found plenty of possible interruptions or errors. The tension in the room subsided as the men were dismissed for sleep. This was only the first session and Moshe was taking it easy on the men. Ben was thankful as he trudged to his bunk and reclined, craving sleep more than anything — deep slumber where he could forget the mission for a few hours. But sleep did not come easily. The racing thoughts in his mind would not stop.

Lara's shirt served as his pillowcase. He buried his face into it, inhaling her scent. For a split-second he felt as if she was there with him, and the longing for her began anew. He pulled the blanket over his body and curled into a fetal position fully dressed. When he wasn't focused like a laser beam on the mission, his mind wandered back to her. What was she doing now? He imagined she was up because it was 9:00 AM where she was. He glanced at his phone. It was 2:00 AM. He closed his eyes for a moment, then picked up the phone and let it ring through.

"Hey, mystery man." Lara answered, and he felt his pulse race.

"I love you, darlin," was all he could manage to say. For some reason he was overcome with emotion. And, he hated the uncontrollable feeling when he was on the verge of tears. He swallowed hard and managed to whisper, "Miss you."

"I miss you, too. Be safe." Lara's voice wavered. He could tell the phone call was even harder for her. He imagined her face wrought with concern and her green eyes filled with sorrow. She added, "I love you so much, Ben, it hurts." Imagining tears filling her eyes, he wanted more than ever to console her, tell her everything would be fine. But he couldn't say the words he knew she wanted to hear, due to the tightness in his throat.

"I know. I miss you, too. I'll be thinking of you. I love you. Gotta go, darlin." He wanted to linger but hung up instead. For a minute, he scrolled through the photos of her on his phone. Damn. He had to be some sort of idiot to be on the other side of the world from someone he loved so much, the woman of his dreams. Why he had this drive, this interminable force within him, to do this *thing* he could not explain. It was as if this was etched into his DNA. He was soon to be thirty-four.

How much longer could he keep up with the young guys, fresh out of training, full of courage, with ripped bodies, sharper skills?

And what was this doing to Lara? Tearing her up inside, he knew. She put on a good front and wasn't crying in front of him as she did at first. But there was a short shelf-life on any relationship that involved extended absences over a long period of time. *She would learn to live without him.* The thought of that nearly tore his heart out. He wanted her to need him, to want him, every hour of every day for the rest of her life. There was nothing more precious to him than her. He had waited all of his life to find her. She was everything he desired and more. He couldn't bear the thought of another man taking his place.

Thinking back over the past year, he came close to losing it when she spent all of that time with Hawk. Even in death, Hawk held a special place in Lara's heart that Ben could never compete with. Hawk had saved her life. And even though he was grateful to the man, he envied the way Lara kept his personal effects at the bungalow, and once caught her wearing Hawk's old denim work coat after he died. She had lowered her eyes and removed it. But he remembered the way she caressed the garment, brushing it lightly with her fingertips, how she slipped it onto the hanger and closed the closet door. He had interrupted her reverie and felt awkward for a second. It was at that moment the realization struck him: Lara had loved Hawk like he loved his brothers. They watched each other's backs. *It was that kind of love.* Something special, unique. It defied explanation. She couldn't part with the memory of Hawk, just as he memorialized Javier and Sam.

Sleep overcame him and his dreams were all about Lara, the beach at Clearwater Farm and the sailboat. He specifically wanted to dream about the sailboat and turned his last thoughts to it, meditating on the image of making love to her below deck, above deck, and everywhere in between. She would be beautiful in the fading sunlight after a long day of sailing.

Chapter 3

Lara's first instinct had been to grab her gun, grab Monique, and head towards the nearest police station. However, she had no proof that the Mustang was following her, although she strongly suspected it was. At this moment, her thoughts turned to Monique and how overwrought she already was. Don't over-react. Lara's suspicions would remain managed for the time being. There was no need to put undue stress on her friend. She needed a plan and thought about the things Ben had taught her. Lara had defended herself in the past. She had beaten up and even killed her share of predators. If she had to, what was one or two more, especially in the name of self-defense?

All she could think about was hearing Ben's voice on that phone call. It might be the last time she heard his voice for days. At least she knew he was alive. That small piece of knowledge gave her a glimmer of hope. She didn't want to look at it that way, but it was the first thought that crossed her mind. If she lost him, she didn't know what she'd do. Ben had become the one steady, reliable, entity in her life. He made her see beauty, where once she saw nothing but harsh reality bathed in cynicism.

To say she missed Ben would be like saying she missed breathing. The anxiety she suffered while he was away was nearly unbearable. She was still raw with the loss of Eliot and Hawk, then Jake. But for Ben's sake, Lara knew she had to be his rock -- just as he was hers.

Monique had spent the night, and Lara was hoping to find something to distract her for another day. She'd drag Monique to the dojo with Don Henderson. It helped Lara with her loneliness, it was time to show Monique how to do the same. As her friend and intern traipsed down the stairway barefoot, Lara teased her.

"You look like you had a good night's rest; your hair looks like you've been in a mosh pit!" Lara joked. At least she got a smile out of Monique.

"Yes, I'm a mess." Monique yawned, "How long did I sleep? My goodness, its 9:00 AM!"

"The plan for the day is to go to the dojo and kick someone's ass." Lara offered. "Trust me, you need to do this."

"Let me eat breakfast first," Monique responded. "How about cereal?"

Lara put the cereal box and milk in front of Monique. "Just don't eat too much, you'll vomit. The workout at the dojo is rigorous. I'm just telling you that from experience." Lara smiled. "And, don't bother to take a shower now, you'll need it later."

Lara tapped her phone and Don Henderson's number came up. His voice boomed over the speaker, "Hey, where the hell have you been? I've been looking for you."

She laughed. "We are heading your way...that is Monique and I are both coming."

"Good." Don was smiling. She could tell from his voice. "I've got two new guys here, young ones. They will give you girls a run for your money. I will supervise."

"See you in a few," Lara replied and ended the call. "There, you see, Monique, you are going to be busy for the next few hours learning some new skills. Let's go."

Within thirty minutes, the two women were in Lara's vehicle and driving into the parking lot at the dojo. For Lara it was like old home week. The regular crowd was there, but she missed Bettencourt's smiling face. So did Monique. Ushered by Don, the two new guys came out to greet them.

"Girls, I want you to meet Tim Crosby and Aaron Brown. Gentlemen, meet Lara and Monique." While Don was being gracious, Lara's eyes roamed over both of these characters. Tim was staring at Monique. Aaron extended his hand to her. She immediately responded. "Great to meet both of you. Let's do the basic stuff today for Monique. She's new."

Tim and Aaron exchanged a glance and said, "Sure, we'll go through the basic class today."

The two looked enough alike to be brothers, but they weren't. Tim was tall and lanky, very muscular with dark brown hair and dark eyes. Aaron had the same coloring but weighed more. But of the two, Lara figured Aaron had more strength, even though Tim was a bit taller. They both looked like they were right out of high school, but she knew they were probably in their early twenties. She guessed they might be college students.

Lara and Monique excused themselves to change in the women's locker room. Lara brought an extra pair of yoga pants for Monique and a loose shirt. "This is adequate, believe me," Lara said.

Once suited up, they met in one of the private rooms with one mirrored wall. Form was everything in mixed martial arts. A spin or a kick executed in front of a mirror could help reveal your flaws or highlight proper technique.

As Lara guessed, Tim took Monique and Aaron faced her. His brown eyes met hers and he smiled. "You've done this before," Aaron stated.

"Yes, I'm a regular," Lara replied. "But I want Monique to start out slowly."

"But that doesn't mean *we* have to..." Aaron said with the beginning of a grin on his face. It was almost as if he was taking Bettencourt's place, goading her.

"All right," Lara said. "Bring it." And the two of them moved to the other side of the room, giving Tim and Monique enough space to practice.

Aaron crouched and circled her. He dove forward, wrapped his hands behind her ankle tendon, and use his shoulder to leverage her down to the ground, and from there had her in a leg-lock. She wasn't ready, damn it, and fell on her ass which served as a wake-up call. She hurled silent insults at herself for not making the dojo a priority lately. She had lost her ability to anticipate her opponent's first strike. *Not good.*

"No worries," Aaron said with a self-confident smile. For the next few minutes he evaded and responded to her every move with well-honed defensive techniques.

But before he could get another sentence out, Lara was prowling around him, back and forth, closer and closer until she caught his arm and flipped him over her hip. It felt good to do that. Maybe the little squirt would stop smiling at her. He bounced up in a flash and tried to tackle her again, but she sidestepped and wrapped her arm around his skull, in a headlock, then jerked him down upon the mat. Aaron fought against her, and he was strong, but Lara kept her grip on him and tightened the vise a little – her legs were out in front of her, and she was sitting up, he was face down on the ground, with her elbow in the back of his neck. She felt Aaron squirm beneath her body, then suddenly he tapped out.

After forty minutes of practice, Monique was talking to herself. She definitely had some moves to memorize. Once in the women's locker room alone, she looked at Lara in the mirror. "Holy shit, you put that guy down in there."

"Yes, and he didn't expect it." Lara smiled, "That was the best part."

"How long before you think I can do that?" Monique asked wide-eyed.

"Maybe a year if you stick to it and come at least twice a week," Lara said, "I'll come with you."

"I want to be able to do that." Monique said smiling. "I *really* do."

Both women showered, dried their hair and made themselves presentable. As Lara and Monique strolled down the hallway to see Don Henderson, Aaron and Tim were taking on new victims in the private lesson room. Don's office door was ajar and Lara tapped on it.

"Hey, girls – how was it? Did these guys do okay? I watched for a while in the two-way mirror." Don waved for them to sit down. "I kept an eye on you in there. Lara, you're a little out of practice but you bounced back. I hope to see you girls here more often."

"Aaron and Tim did a great job." Lara said.

Monique added, "I had fun. I'll be back. Where do I sign?"

Don put the forms in front of Monique and turned to Lara. "How's Ben? Haven't seen him for a while."

Lara smiled, "He's on a trip, but it's not a long one. Hey, how about you and Olivia coming over for dinner tonight? I can make lobster."

Don seemed delighted. He called Olivia and she was enthusiastic. "Great what time do you want us there?"

Lara thought for a moment. "How about 6:00 PM, is that too early?"

"No, that's great." Don waved goodbye as they left. Lara was thrilled to be having Don and Olivia over for dinner. Monique would enjoy their company, that's if she could convince her to stay. Plus, dinner would be one more distraction. Lara was thinking of lunch and an after-Christmas shopping trip for the next few hours.

Outside in the parking lot, Monique elbowed Lara, "Hey, isn't that the car you called Bettencourt about?" The Mustang was there, covered with flat black paint, and low profile racing tires. Lara jotted down the plate number and stopped by the police station on the way home.

Paul Simpson, a tall blonde officer who looked like he was right out of the police academy, smiled, "How can I help you ladies?"

"I'm Randall Bettencourt's fiancée," Monique started. She gave Bettencourt's old badge number, and one or two of his former colleagues in order to confirm who she was, and who Bettencourt was.

"We need to know who owns this vehicle, it's been following us for several days." Lara said flatly, handing him the piece of paper. "Bettencourt said you could help."

Simpson moved the women to a side room and closed the door. "Let me see that." He smiled and said he'd be right back. Lara glanced at Monique nervously. The two sat in the small interrogation room silently, not moving but mentally twitching.

Simpson was back in a flash. "It's registered to an Aaron Brown." Monique and Lara exchanged the same look, one of surprise followed by alarm.

"Damn, it's the guy I just threw down at the dojo," Lara exhaled. "Can you give me his address and whatever information you have? I'll take it from there."

Lara noticed Simpson's eyes narrowed. She guessed what he was thinking: Bettencourt's fiancée came in with her friend, asking about a car, and the friend says that she would handle it? That was a Hell and a No. "May I ask what this is about?"

"No thanks, we've got this." She pulled Monique by the sleeve and thanked Officer Simpson, "We've got to go."

In the parking lot, Lara started her Mercedes and simultaneously tapped her phone. Rusty's voice boomed over the speaker in the car. "Hey, Lara, what are you up to?"

"I need to see you. It's business." Lara said tersely.

"Yup, come up to the range. I'm here this afternoon." Rusty seemed to know something was up. "I'll see you when you get here." The phone call blipped off.

"One more little detail." Lara was talking to herself and Monique was listening. Lara took a device out of the console that looked like a magnet and made a U-turn to return to the dojo parking lot. The Mustang was parked and no one was around as Lara slipped out of her vehicle. She bent down with the pretense of picking up her glove from the ground, as she tucked the magnetic device to the underside of the black car.

"I don't dare to ask you what that was all about." Monique said as they pulled out of the parking lot into traffic.

Lara tapped her phone and found the app she was looking for. She handed the phone to Monique. "It's a tracking device. I want to know where these guys are at all times. But more than that, I want to know *who the hell they are* and why they've been following us. Rusty will get to the bottom of it."

The Mercedes raced through city traffic and was soon on the outskirts moving in the general direction toward Panther Pond. Rusty's domicile was really a compound on nine acres, combination shooting range, secret bunker, and Lara's home away from home. As Lara stepped out of the Mercedes after a forty-five minute drive, she inhaled the fresh clean air and her eyes soaked in the raw beauty of the frozen pond. A January thaw was beginning. For a moment the stillness was complete, only interrupted by the occasional twitter of birds. Unlike the seaside home she lived in, Rusty's place on the pond was incredibly quiet. No rolling waves here. Dead silence.

It was Monique's first time on the pond. "Wow, this place is awesome."

"I think you'll like it." Lara smiled as they trudged toward the cabin on the edge of the pond. "It's rustic but charming, and there's always a crackling fire going."

Rusty met them at the door with a smile, his hair tousled but the familiar Red Sox baseball cap covered most of it. His thick soft chamois shirt was frayed, but Lara loved the feel of it when she hugged him. Rusty was her go-to guy, her step-father, but more importantly he had a network of spies, ex-FBI spooks, who could gather information on just about anyone on the face of the earth. He would come in handy today.

"What brings you girls out here?" He drew them inside and bolted the door.

"We're being followed."

~ Ben ~

Mock-ups were performed during the day and the team was fully loaded. While in Israel, they worked in a protected alley and simulated the hits they practiced on the computer game. Then took a brief break for lunch and a nap. The nighttime mock-up was critical. It closely resembled what would really take place if all went according to plan.

"Old man, you are keeping up well," Moshe slapped Ben's back laughing.

Ben gave him a smile, "I'm preserving some of my energy for tonight. It will be a long one."

"Wisdom trumps youth every time, my friend." Moshe said with a somber tone. "Use it -- your wisdom. You are the best frogman I've ever seen, and I've seen quite a few in my time." Ben stared into Moshe's black eyes, they reminded him of black olives. He reached around Moshe's narrow back and tousled his thick black hair, knowing it was a source of irritation for his lanky friend. Moshe growled good-naturedly, then punched Ben's shoulder.

"Yeah, I know, I'm great." Ben taunted Moshe. The two entered the dining facility jousting, but the conversation turned serious. "I'm concerned about this coming intelligence leak the community has been talking about. It may jeopardize this mission." Ben whispered to Moshe.

"I'm watching for it, bro." Moshe's eyes met his. "There's an entire wing of computer nerds back at the office looking for the leak, when and if it hits. It's my biggest concern, too. I have full faith this team can take out the targets, but it will be much more difficult if the targets are tipped off beforehand, or if our human intelligence working on the ground are exposed. Leaking this information could change everything. Why are Americans allowing this to happen? Tell me this. Make me understand why they want to commit suicide, using us as the pawns?"

"I wish I could explain it." Ben began, "But the only reason it is being done is greed, ego, power, revenge. These are the passions driving American politics now, and it's putting the United States in grave danger. Those in power have lost sight that without the protection and survival of America, *nothing else matters*." Ben said with a heavy sigh. "I wish I could change that, but it's why I left the Navy. I have to do things on my terms or not at all. I couldn't deal with the politically correct bullshit any longer. The sensitivity training, calling Islam a religion, when it's Nazi ideology plain and simple. The state department won't even go into Islamic compounds because they haven't declared radical Islamists as terror groups. Hell, those at the top won't even use the words *Islamic terrorists*. Political correctness will be the end of us all. Either that, or we end them first."

Immersed in a wave of anger, Ben continued, "Terrorists have figured out how to use the freedoms in America to their favor. They are using immigration loopholes to their advantage, and enjoy the protection that comes with being an American citizen. Hell, they even use our court system with tax-funded lawyers to defend them. Hard working American people pay to defend jihadists. Veterans returning from fighting these bastards in wars are paying for their rights. The State Department gives religious protection to radical terrorists trying to kill us. It's high level insanity."

Exhaling, Ben knew Moshe had heard this rant before. But he believed every word of it. He wasn't just blowing off steam. He feared his own country was going into an unstoppable decline, and it was his duty to try to stop it, in any way that he could.

After dinner, the nighttime mock-up began and lasted well into the morning hours. Exhausted and hungry, the men ate and crawled into their beds. Beneath the ground in the bunker, there was no sound except for the soft whir of the ductwork purifying the air. It was soothing and quiet in his room once the men had fallen asleep. So quiet he could hear his heart beating. He recognized his insomnia was worse than ever on this mission. It was the inability to control what might happen that kept him awake. *Those who hired him seemed to be the ones who might become his undoing.* Ego was always at the center of all evil. It wasn't about the techniques used or who was spying on whom. *The bottom line was survival of the fittest. When the hell would these stupid politicians get it?* There were no rules in battle. This was a brave new world, and the political hacks were living in a bubble, making arguments that were moot upon the battlefield.

After days of practice and communication with human intel on the ground, Moshe ordered the C-130J stocked and ready for take-off. The team was in good spirits and Ben found it difficult to be his usual jovial self. Although he smiled and grabbed arms and slapped backs as always, he did not share the worries lurking in the back of his mind. It would be a night flight, and the men were happy to have the chance to sleep for the fifteen hour trip.

They were wheels-up by 9:00 PM and landed in Soto Cano Air Base, Honduras at noon the following day. Soto Cano was the location of the U.S. Southern Command. A Joint Task Force-Bravo operated forward, USSOCOM's area of responsibility encompassed thirty-one countries and ten territories, thus covering close to one-sixth of the landmass of the earth.

The humidity hit him like a wall the moment Ben stepped off the plane. It would take a day or two for his body to acclimate, and the men had filled up on water enhanced with electrolytes in preparation for what lie ahead. A convoy of heavily armored vehicles swept the team to their temporary housing in a bunker beneath the base. There, they were brought into a room and fitted with the newest forward-deployed TALOS exoskeleton suits, a thin liquid body-armor for protection, and unique goggles that not only allowed night vision, but acted as an undetectable communication device, simply known as G's. The goggles were a full-color, 3D heads-up display that provided rapid, real-time battlefield knowledge. With a high-resolution transparent display, the eyeglasses overlaid a data and a video stream giving the men full view of the battle around them. Aside from enhancing night vision, the G's provided waypoints, routing information, and the ability to identify hostile and friendly forces, track personnel and assets, and coordinate small unit actions.

Piling into the war room, Moshe ran the team through the first strike. The Dark Horse war game was up on the screen and each man participated in some way, utilizing their unique skills. Getting ready for these targets was the biggest challenge. Ben's worry was: There were just too many variables. The Latin American police state was not friendly and there was a strong narco-terrorist element that would surround them. The one thing he hated more than anything else was uncertainty and now he would be immersed in it.

Before the game ended, Moshe made an announcement that caused Ben even more anxiety.

"Sorry to say, guys, that two of the bastards that were on our radar, have managed to slip away in Guatemala. There were five of them in one location and two have just been reported missing. Our HUMINT on the ground are trying to locate them without being obvious. Chief, it will be up to you to find them, and we will stand-by to provide you with every technological or personnel need possible. Now hit the sack. Tomorrow is going to be a long hot day."

Chapter 4

~ Lara ~

Lara didn't want her friend to go home. Monique was as concerned as she was about their husbands' mission. Lara was not alone with her worries about Ben. Monique was somewhere else in deep thought. What was Ben doing and would she really *want* to know? She knew he was reluctant to take on this mission, but why was it different from all the others? She had no answers. The questions cycled through her mind repeatedly, leaving her exhausted with worry. And, now she had the added worry of someone following her. Rusty was doing a complete background check on the two young men, but Lara's anxiety was at an all-time high.

They drove home in silence awaiting Rusty's information. She fingered her Glock and even wore the weapon inside the house utilizing an oversized sweatshirt to keep it hidden. As silly as it seemed to carry inside the house, the little voice in the back of her mind reminded her she was being watched. Curtains were drawn and she tried to focus on the coming evening.

There were several things keeping her from just running to the nearest bunker – the first being: she didn't want to be followed. Plus, the threat level wasn't clear. So far, Rusty hadn't found anything earth-shattering about Aaron Brown or Tim Crosby. There was a breaking and entering charge and some other misdemeanors. He would continue digging, but there wasn't anything that told her to run for her life just yet. With the information at hand, it could be less a matter of being stalked, and more a matter of being cased. She had a nice house, in a nice neighborhood, and with Brown's resume of breaking into homes, he could have been a mere criminal.

And if that was the case, then Brown was going to have a big problem awaiting him if he was doing reconnaissance for a burglary.

If Brown was more than that ... Lara felt a spark of rage within her. It blossomed from her stomach and enveloped her chest. When the shot of adrenaline hit, she felt the buzz, and had to stop moving for a moment to take a deep breath. Steady. Think, plan, then act; don't react. Hope for the best, but plan for the worst. Ben's words lived in her brain. Even though she hadn't killed someone in a while, she was ready, willing and able.

She cleaned the house in anticipation of having Don and Olivia over for dinner. They hadn't been to Clearwater Farm since the Christmas gathering. She could not let Monique go home. She didn't want to frighten her, but Lara knew the danger she could be in if Brown were more than a simple criminal. The two women didn't talk about it in detail, but Lara knew Monique's anxiety level was as high, if not higher, than her own. There were times when Monique would be unusually quiet or somber. Lara recognized the faraway look in her eyes and left her alone for a while. The human mind required time and space to process this kind of stress. This much, Lara knew firsthand.

Knowing that Don liked casual fare, with Monique's help, she arranged the dinner table in the kitchen. Nothing formal for these two. Einstein was bumping his nose against her shin repeatedly, nudging her to feed him. This dog was better than an alarm clock. She smiled and poured the cup of organic dog food into his bowl, which he proceeded to eat with gusto.

As she cleaned out his water bowl her phone chimed. It was the alert she had assigned for Ben's phone, and the moment she heard it her heart nearly stopped. She put the bowl of water on the floor and grabbed her phone, "Ben?"

There was a delay on the satellite phone but she heard his voice with the slight Irish inflection, "Darlin? Oh good. I'm glad I caught you. How are you? I miss you. But you know that. What are you doing?"

To hear his voice brought tears to her eyes, but she'd never let him know, "I'm great...in fact, making dinner for Don and Olivia. How are you?"

"Everything is fine on this end. Not to worry. Did you check out those guys following you? Make sure you see Rusty." His voice trailed off.

"Yes. So far, it appears these two are petty criminals. I won't panic just yet. But, I'm carrying and ready. I don't want you to worry about me. You've got enough on your mind." She breathed.

"Damn, I wish I was there, with you, darlin. Going into another phase right now, but I have a good feeling about things. I just wanted to hear your voice. I can't wait to see you, darlin, coming home is always the best part and it's all I can think about. I love you." Ben said with a serious tone. She heard voices in the background and what sounded like vehicles starting up. "Got to go, darlin – tell me you love me."

She felt her voice crack as she said the words, "I love you, Ben…" and the phone went silent. She knew he was locked and loaded to go somewhere, because she heard the engines. But, more than that, it was the anticipatory tone of his voice she had heard many times before. *The important thing was: he was alive, right now.* Reason enough to smile and secretly celebrate tonight with Don and Olivia.

She turned and looked at Monique, "It was Ben. He just called me out of the blue."

"Bettencourt just called me, too." Monique sounded hopeful, almost like her old self. Then her forehead wrinkled with concern. "Maybe there's something going on…something terrible…and they're saying goodbye."

Lara arched a brow. "Did he actually say goodbye?"

"No …" she said hesitantly.

"Then you can't think like that. They're just taking off and checking in. That's all." Lara said it with such conviction she almost convinced herself.

Monique answered the door as she noticed Don and Olivia approaching. Although she seemed worried, Monique appeared a bit uplifted by Bettencourt's phone call. Lara sensed a positive quality in Ben's voice. She forced a smile as she hugged Don and Olivia. She had painstakingly prepared a diabetic-friendly dinner for Don. She missed their meetings at Pancake Heaven, but both of their lives had changed since she married Ben. Monique was smiling and petting Einstein, a very good sign. And, Don and Olivia were verbally sparring with one another, which was normal for them.

As they enjoyed dinner, Don smiled, "You girls are certainly in a good mood. Aren't your husbands both away?"

"Yes," Lara interjected. "They're on a hunting trip, but will be back soon. It's a safari type of thing." Monique smiled and nodded, not uttering a word. "It's good for them to get away like that," Lara continued.

Lara knew that Don was aware the men were on a mission, and the details would not be discussed. So, he talked about business at the dojo and the new employees there. "Aaron and Tim are doing a wonderful job, don't you think?"

"They seem to be highly skilled." Lara replied. "I'd love to know more about them. How did you meet these guys?

Don ran his hand over his face. "I placed an ad on the website. Nothing special. Those two showed up on my doorstep the very next day. They said they really wanted the job and demonstrated their ability on the spot. I had them fill out an application and hired them. They said they had applied for a few other jobs. They're college kids."

"Did you do background checks on them?" Lara asked.

"You know, I remember giving that to Vivian to do, but now that you mention it...I don't remember if she gave me anything on them."

"Just so you know, one of them has a record." Lara leaned in, "And they've been following us in that blacked-out Mustang."

Don's eyes locked with hers. "You're kidding, right?"

"No. Take a look." Lara handed over the information from Rusty.

Don's facial expression became somber, then apologetic. "Damn it, Lara. I should've been much more careful. These guys are following you? I'll take them down. Damn it! This is my fault."

"Let me handle it, Don. I just wanted you to know about this. Maybe it's best if you don't let on right away." Lara tapped her phone and brought up the tracking app. "There they are….down the road from us right now."

Don stared at the phone. "Jesus - let's go get them, right now. Call the police."

"The police know about this, sort of. I've been there, and got some basic information from an officer, so Rusty could do some digging. If they try anything, I'm ready." Lara lifted her sweatshirt showing him the holstered Glock.

"Oh Lara, that's too dangerous." Olivia exclaimed.

"I know what I'm doing," Lara declared. "I know what the laws are. I would follow the law."

"I think we should stay here with you tonight." Olivia suggested.

Lara now wondered if she should have told them about Aaron and Tim, but decided she had to let them know. No telling what might have happened if she didn't; and she couldn't take that chance.

"Okay, we don't want to make this overly dramatic. We don't know why they're following us. It could be less nefarious than we've imagined. And, you're not sleeping over. You're staying for dessert and decaf coffee. I want you to keep me company for a little longer.

They agreed. Monique seemed more comfortable. Lara exhaled. Glancing at her phone she watched the blinking dot on the map, but realized those in the vehicle could be walking around the property right now without her knowledge. She excused herself to use the bathroom and stepped into Ben's office to examine the security cameras around the perimeter. Playing back the video she viewed it searching for any sign of movement. Then double checked the perimeter alarm on her phone. It was on. For a moment the hair on the back of her neck prickled, and she reflexively put her hand on the gun at her hip. The hairs were a sign Ben taught her early on to notice. Hackles, he called it, a primitive survival mechanism in the human body. Her hackles were being raised and she wasn't about to ignore it.

As she moved back into the kitchen, the subject of Don's nephew, Eric, came up. The last time Lara had seen Eric was at the completion of his landscaping project. She had been using photos of the renovation of the purple Victorian on her website. It was a sight to behold.

"Eric has a girlfriend now." Don informed them. "She seems to be a nice girl. She loves the purple Victorian, especially that garden, Lara, it is beautiful." For a moment there was a pause in the conversation and Lara knew everyone at the table immediately thought about Hawk. She remembered the loving care he took landscaping the show-stopper. Lara felt a pang of sorrow, but stuffed it away.

After a moment, Lara broke the uncomfortable silence. "I'm happy for Eric. He deserves to have a life and I wish nothing but the best for him."

Lara knew Don sensed her grief about Hawk. Don was one of those guys who would probe and prod, wanting to soothe her somehow, wanting to fix it. "I know you must miss Hawk every time you walk into that bungalow. Damn awful how he was killed. That son-of-a-bitch that shot him thought he was Ben. Jesus. That was something awful."

"Yes," Lara exhaled. Her right hand moved mindlessly up and down her leg, the edge of her palm brushed against the holster every time it slid up. "Hawk is there, at the bungalow, in spirit. I kept the few personal items he owned right where he left them. I know it sounds silly, but when I take a break from work and the place is quiet, it's as if Hawk is there with me, sort of a Jiminy Cricket sitting on my shoulder, telling me everything is going to be all right."

Olivia chimed in, "Well, he *was* your Jiminy Cricket. Hawk saved your life when you first moved in here. He beat the crap out of that guy that attacked you, almost killed him. Hawk put him in the hospital for a long time. You've done wonderfully with all that's happened, Lara. You're a strong person. We know you miss Hawk -- he was a great guy."

Monique interrupted the mini-eulogy to Hawk, "Hey, do you guys want these fresh berries with whipped cream? There's plenty here."

After dinner, they moved into the living room. Lara's eyes were drawn to the large window framing Casco Bay and the ocean beyond. Even in the darkness, her eyes could make out the outline of Fort Gorges, a place she and William studied on the internet. Built of granite, the fort sat on Hog's Ledge and had been there since the 1800's. Ben had said it was fitting for a former Navy man to have a fort in front of his residence; he was fascinated by it, too.

All she could think of was Ben whenever she scanned the sea; he loved it so. It was such a part of his life. She was facing west and the sun had already set. The strangest feeling crept over her that Ben was somewhere near the ocean, suffering and perspiring, nearly suffocating from the heat. Why she felt that, she couldn't say. It was a fleeting image.

She turned to her guests. "Okay, who wants to play a couple of hands of poker?"

Lara broke out the card table. When she took her seat, she slid her gun into her lap as inconspicuously as possible. The poker game ensued. Don made a few mistakes leaving him wide open for Monique to clean up the table. Olivia started teasing him as they played a few more hands. Before long, tears streamed down their faces as they snorted and giggled. It felt good to lose control for a little while with people you loved and trusted.

Even though Lara was laughing, she couldn't shake the apprehension that lurked in the corner of her mind. She hoped that Ben was safe and sound and that the black Mustang was gone. But as she glanced at her phone, the flashing dot remained. Underneath the table she sent a text to Officer Simpson. He'd given her his phone number if anything funny happened and this fit that description. She figured the squad car would cruise by and spook the Mustang. Or, at least she hoped that's what would happen. In the safety of her home, she was behind several reinforced doors, and locks that rivaled the security of a bank vault.

She continued playing cards, but couldn't stop thinking about Ben. Hunting terrorists was much more dangerous than any real-life safari. She knew the CIA only sent him after the most dangerous men, hell-bent on destroying her husband. The images that ran through her mind constantly were horrific. Although Ben wore disguises and spoke the dialect, there was always the chance he could be captured and killed. She imagined how the U.S. government would disavow even knowing who he was if he was paraded on YouTube for a beheading video. There would be no cavalry to save her husband if that situation developed. She pushed the image away and tried to focus on the game and the people in front of her.

Don and Olivia were chuckling. Monique was, too. The poker game was a silly distraction and she allowed herself to be swept away in the craziness of it for a while longer. She couldn't stop living, although she felt she couldn't exhale until Ben returned. And the evil thoughts intruded at the most inconvenient times.

"I've got to take the dog outside," Lara announced. Don insisted on going with her. They stood side by side as Einstein wandered in the yard, the security lights highlighted his dark body against the white snow. Lara glanced at her phone and the flashing dot remained. "Back inside." Lara spoke to Einstein and he trotted through the doorway with her. Although it was early, everyone was tired. Lara hugged Don and Olivia and watched as they got into Don's truck and drove away. The red dot on her phone remained stationary as her guests drove away.

Lara glanced at Monique in the kitchen. "Hot cocoa would be good right now."

"A big one, with marshmallow?" Monique asked.

"Yes. And I have a good movie to watch, we'll turn out the lights." Lara started making the hot chocolate they both loved. Einstein wagged his tail. "And, a treat for you, buddy! " Lara handed him a brand new chew toy with a squeaker and Einstein was in heaven.

"He loves those things," Monique observed.

"Oh yes, he keeps chewing it until the squeaker doesn't work." Lara laughed.

"He's a lot of company for you, isn't he?" Monique sat on the sofa.

"He's Ben's dog. I feel like Ben is here with me just a little bit when I have Einstein here." Lara confessed. She rubbed her hand over his egg-shaped bull-dog head.

"I love dogs." Monique said plaintively.

"Let's visit some breeders in the next few days. What type of dog do you want?" Lara suggested.

"I had a Golden Retriever when I was a kid, but she died. Her name was Brandy." Monique said.

"Well, let's find some Golden Retriever puppies. It would be so much fun." Lara smiled.

"Yes." Monique agreed. "Let's do it."

The sound outside that initially sounded like firecrackers startled Lara. She grabbed Monique, and the two women hit the floor in the kitchen as the dog cowered beneath the table.

"Damn it." Lara muttered. "That's gunfire. Don't move off this floor."

Lara's phone rang and it was Officer Simpson. "Mrs. Keegan..." He paused, as though he was out of breath. "It's me, Simpson. I'm right ... outside your door." As Lara opened the door, Officer Simpson fell forward onto the floor of her kitchen.

"Oh God, he's been shot!" Monique screamed.

Lara drew her Glock in a two-handed stance and dropped to one knee, staring out into the night. She cautiously reached up to turn off the kitchen light so she wouldn't be backlit. "Monique, bring him inside!"

Monique crawled forward on her belly. She grabbed Simpson's arm and pulled, using her legs to push off against the doorframe, giving her enough leverage to bring him further inside. Lara reached down to slide Simpson's legs out of the way just enough to close the door. Her eyes never left the darkness.

Instinctively, Lara tried to render aid to the fallen officer. "Call 911, get an ambulance!" she said to Monique. Simpson was bleeding profusely on the floor. The shot was straight through his back. She knew it hit his heart or lungs. After a few frantic minutes the sound of Simpson's labored breathing stopped and his eyes became lifeless. He was gone. Lara crawled to Ben's office and watched the security screens for better detail. When she saw nothing there, she looked at her phone. The flashing dot had left the vicinity and was moving rapidly north. *Bastards!* They'd killed Simpson and now they were getting away.

She called the police station, gave her name, address, Simpson's badge number, and said, "Shots fired. Officer down at my location. The shooters are at the intersection of Route 9 and Route 111 right now!"

"Ma'am, how are you—"

"Don't ask me how I know, I'm tracking them. Just get them!"

"Stay on the line."

Monique was crying softly as she cradled Officer Simpson's head in her lap. Einstein was shivering under the table. Lara felt helpless and angry in the same moment. She wanted more than ever to jump into her Mercedes and track them down and kill them herself, but then realized that's exactly what they wanted her to do. No. She had to be calculating with her next move. They needed to come to her. She began to formulate a plan.

Lara chastised herself silently. She had been arrogant and bold, not making a formal police report. She didn't want to tip off the bastards following her. Because of her actions, she felt responsible for the events that played out. Officer Simpson had paid the ultimate price. She was going to rectify that as best she could. She watched the red flashing dot on her phone while incredible frustration consumed her.

Rusty was trying to call her and she toggled off the police station call to answer. "Lara, I've got some answers for you...can you talk?"

"Actually, I'm on the phone with the police right now. They're in pursuit of the Mustang. The bastards shot a young police officer though the back. He's lying here dead in my kitchen. I'll call you back." Her finger shook as she picked up the police call. "They've turned North onto Route 111." She gave the police an accurate account of the vehicle's movements, hoping they could catch them.

The police lagged far behind the Mustang. The flashing red dot was moving at a high rate of speed. The dot took a northerly route onto unpaved roads, and plunged deeper into the wooded wilderness. Then, something strange happened – the red dot disappeared. The device could have been hit with force by a flying rock or somehow detached from the Mustang. But the end result was: they got away. She felt sick to her stomach as she dialed Rusty back. "Yeah, I'm here. They got away. What do you have?"

"Details. Aaron Brown is working for a terrorist by the name of Abdul Rahman Shafir. The NSA has extensive Twitter conversations between the two. It looks like this guy is part of a sleeper cell here in the states. And, here's the really bad part: his mission is to find Ben Keegan and capture or kill him. If he can't find Keegan, he was ordered to find his wife or another family member and hold them. Lara this isn't good."

While Rusty was talking, Lara clutched her stomach, ran to the sink and vomited. The police were at the door with Monique. Several first responders arrived. Lara watched as they lovingly carried Officer Simpson's lifeless body out to the waiting van.

"Lara, are you there?"

Rusty had been talking the entire time, but she felt as if she was in some surreal horror movie.

"Yes, I'm here. I'm enraged. Why weren't we informed of this by the feds? Oh God, Rusty...if I hadn't called the police, that bullet in Simpson would've been in me." She closed her eyes as Monique put her arm around her shoulder.

"They've been stalking you, waiting for the opportunity to snatch you up." Rusty continued. "You've got to get out of there. They know where you live. It's time to take a short trip."

Lara took several deep breaths as she watched the police take Simpson's body away and process the scene. Her eyes narrowed, and her breathing sped up a little. She felt the rage return. The rage she felt since she was first raped. Her response to being helpless again. Whenever someone wanted to take away her choices, her freedom, her future, her first response was to lash out.

And she wanted these men dead at her feet.

But one thing at a time.

"I've got a better idea. Let's set them up. I want to capture them. They probably have a wealth of information."

"Too dangerous." Rusty murmured. "But, they can follow your vehicle and someone in it who *looks like you*. I'm coming over and bringing a friend with me. Sit tight."

Chapter 5

Guatemala

~ Ben ~

The five terrorists Ben hunted in Guatemala were not living in any five-star resorts. Each target was in a different location, two of them had disappeared. The team would split off and lie in wait to quietly pick off bodyguards and then get each target. At least that was the plan. By daybreak, the men were sorted into pairs. Then up-armored Jeeps took them for a five hour ride on bumpy back roads.

The Dark Horse Guardians were impossible to distinguish from the general populace. If anyone stopped them, they looked Guatemalan and were armed to the teeth. It was unlikely that they would be stopped, however, because the men had beards and dressed in old Nike shirts with body armor beneath and cargo pants. They did not look like Navy SEALs, or Americans, for that matter. With dark glasses and bandannas tied around their heads, they resembled runners in the narco trade. They would be given a wide berth if they were stopped by police. Ben already knew what to say to move the authorities off their trail, if it came to that. Each man had thousands of pesos rolled up in his backpack, and plenty of gold coins, just in case. Greasing the palm of a police officer in this part of the world was common practice, actually expected, as a tip would be to a waiter.

During the day, they used their regular coms, commonly called Tactical Ears, miniscule devices that were invisible in the ear canal with a tiny clip inside the collar of their shirts. But at night they'd use the G's. Constant contact was critical in coordinating each hit. Ben and Elvis were paired and riding in the Jeep heading for the rendezvous point, a decrepit inn called The Cabana on the main street of the town of El Chulupa.

Ben had spent time there during work-ups between tours, so he had seen the place up close and personal, and none of it was pretty. Third-world poverty prevailed. The streets were crowded with open markets, donkey carts, cars, and scooters for those at the top of the food chain. It never ceased to amaze him how corruption ruled this sector of the planet. The war on drugs was *called* a war, but there were no battle lines drawn in this parched wilderness. Similarly, the war on terrorism wasn't officially called a war, but the president was killing terrorists with drones and the CIA was hiring black-ops off the books to kill bad guys.

Damn it. *Why didn't the United States know when to declare a real war?* Those running the country he loved were making a mockery of it. Misusing the word *war* had become a joke, like *The War on Drugs* or *The War on Women*. What was taking place in Guatemala was being run the same way as the fake *War on Terror*. Similar to Afghanistan, it didn't take long before he realized he was in a no man's land where the dead piled up in silence and the living had nothing to say. Hordes of beggars and gang members roamed the area seeking food, money or young women to rape. Life was cheap. People were killed for a pair of shoes or a handful of pills.

Ben knew that half of the problem was that wars were not formally declared on people, or organizations. The standard declaration of war was against a nation. No one had the brains to update an act of war against a group of individuals. Then again, even the concept of a massive non-governmental entity like al-Qaeda or the Islamic State wasn't around when the rules for declaring war were written. In his opinion, it was high time to formally declare war on the factions and ideologies they were up against. This wasn't 1935, when war wasn't declared on Fascism or Nazism, but on Italy and Germany. *Changing the concept of war, updating the landscape of the battlefield to include everywhere wasn't exactly a concept most politicians understood.* And, as a result, Islamofascism continued its march unfettered, while politicians who knew nothing about the battle sat in air-conditioned rooms and worried about getting reelected more than protecting the United States.

The other half of the problem was a distinct lack of military knowledge and balls.

Once they reached their destination, Ben and Elvis went inside the inn and were greeted by Paco. The inn was a safe house and Paco led them to the back rooms that looked out onto an alley. A team of twelve human intel personnel had been living in the buildings facing the alley for six months. Malarial mosquitoes, fecal flies, fire ants and numerous other insects competed to set up shop on his body as he stepped outside. The HUMINT men and women worked and lived amongst the people, blending in. Their description of the place had been accurate, he could say that much.

Paco, a young energetic man with dark brown hair spoke in a soft voice, "I'm the innkeeper and you are new tenants, on a narco errand, passing through." Ben swept Paco with his eyes, taking in every detail about him. He appeared alert, energetic, and kind as he handed Ben and Elvis a bottle of fresh water. "Here, drink this bottled water. Everything here is foul. We've got plenty of beer, too." He smiled and his white teeth looked bright against his sweaty tanned skin. He seemed to read Ben's mind as he mopped his forehead, and batted the flies away. Paco chuckled, "You'll get used to the heat after a few days. The flies, not so much."

Ben smiled back, "Hopefully, we will only be here a few days. So, tell me, what's going on?"

Paco recounted the latest skirmish, "Twenty-nine farm workers were decapitated and their heads were strewn across a field a few nights ago, but when I asked questions of the residents, they gave me blank looks and shrugged as if it didn't happen. Two well-known peasant leaders were killed in separate incidents as if by ghosts. It took place in broad daylight, but no witnesses. The people of the community are reluctant to admit it even happened."

Paco continued, "Six Mexicans were shot in the house next door a week ago. A mystery man took away the bodies and the homeowner scrubbed the blood before police arrived. The police decided nothing happened. You need to watch your back here, man, and take plenty of extra ammo in your backpack. It's bad – I mean really bad."

Ben had expected as much. El Chulupa was a sun-blistered one-street town on Guatemala's boundary with Honduras, once in the middle of nowhere, now in the middle of Latin America's drug war. Mexico's drug-fuelled battle left 58,000 dead in the past four years, and continued leaving a trail of bodies in Guatemala and across much of Central America.

Mexico's crackdown pushed some narcos south. In particular, the Zetas, a brutal band of thugs who sought to eliminate rivals and anyone who stood in the way of their business dealings, especially those who attempted to investigate their brutal murders. The Zetas were particularly brutal in that their membership roster involved a heavy presence of former Mexican soldiers. The pay was better – they had started by being paid by the narcos, and then they decided that they would make *much* better money if they *were* the narcos.

Guatemala, Honduras and El Salvador were already world renown for murder due to poverty, gangs and government corruption. Alarm bells rang in Ben's mind. General Peter Frost, head of U.S. SOCOM, had briefed them on Central America's gravest threat, and how the cartels were being welcomed to cross the border into the United States along with terrorists released from Gitmo.

Come one, come all. As if the United States needed any more problems than it already had. There were times he wondered just how corrupt his *own* government was, especially allowing the breach of the U.S. border so willingly. Ben was painfully aware the commander-in-chief's first responsibility was to protect and defend the United States, but he was seeing first-hand the results of ignoring that all-important duty.

On the fly-in, Ben observed dozens of long, cut-outs in the jungle canopy: airstrips for cocaine-filled planes. The aircraft, worth a small fraction of the cargo's street value, were often abandoned and there was an entire cemetery of them, a sort of aviation boneyard. Street children picked over the parts and sold them to anyone who would buy them. On the ground you could travel for days without seeing another soul, but when the forest gave way to pasture and bony cattle it meant a town was coming up. El Chulupa was a five-hour bumpy drive from Soto Cano. It reeked of fear.

Paco warned him, "There are eyes and ears everywhere. Be careful who you talk with. The phones are tapped, so people speak in codes. Terror is palpable when people know they can be killed and there are no consequences."

El Chulupa was quiet, for now. After the beheadings, the government declared a temporary state of emergency in the region, enabling the corrupt army to impose a curfew, chase suspects and feign support of the ineffectual police force. Dozens of vehicles and hundreds of weapons, including assault rifles and grenades, had been impounded. About two dozen Zeta suspects had been rounded up, the usual suspects. The strutting narcos, usually brandishing weapons across their chests, were temporarily in hiding, or locked up being well fed. Through Paco, Ben learned that large-scale human rights violations, war crimes and genocide went unpunished. In Guatemala impunity was the rule, justice an exception.

Welcome to Latin America.

The problem was, the cartels employed most of the residents of the country in one way or another, so no one could really be trusted. A fortune by local standards, the cartels paid a finder's fee as a recruitment tool. But like the mafia, once you got into the gangs, you never got out. The army patrolled with teenagers dressed in khaki and on foot, but the narco-terrorists knew it was a powerless force. Many of the Zetas were former members of Mexican and Guatemalan special-forces, which didn't make Ben feel any better about the mission.

Ben and Elvis slept with one eye open the first night. Once, Ben closed his eyes and pictured Lara lounging on the sofa at home watching television. Although thousands of miles apart, they were almost in the same time zone. Her shirt served as his pillow on the bare mattress in the corner of the room. The sounds in the night were those of babies crying, occasional gun shots, and a few street scuffles outside in the alley.

Elvis slept in the opposite corner of the room with a loaded weapon at the ready. Ben's stomach was empty and he sucked down bottles of water as if he couldn't get enough. Thankfully, the temperature dropped to the 70's at night. But the humidity was non-stop.

The next day they ate at the local cantina and mixed with the residents, telling them they were just passing through. Ben handed out a pack of cigarettes to a few of the locals. Well disguised as Latin Americans, both men seemed to pass the sniff test. Little did those in the cantina know, the coming night would bring another bout of unrest to their dreadful little settlement. Ben and Elvis strolled through town past their target's dwelling absorbing every detail from behind sunglasses as they sauntered by. A ramshackle two-story building painted bright yellow, it housed one of the top Islamic State masterminds.

A woman having the appearance of a housekeeper exited the building. Stout, dark, and wearing an apron, she was all business as she stepped into the street and headed toward the market place around the corner. Once she was out of earshot, Ben and Elvis stopped in front of the building to argue. While they pretended to be fighting with one another, Ben saw a figure hovering in the doorway of the bright yellow building. Elvis shoved his hand into Ben's chest pushing him back a few steps, shouting in Spanish. As they did so, out of the corner of Ben's eye, he observed a figure emerging in broad daylight. It was their target, Mohammed Al Safi.

In the crowded street filled with vendors and hooligans, they ceased arguing but feigned conversation with one another. Ben moved cautiously behind the man as he rapidly strode along the dirt road. Occasionally, Ben squatted to pick up trash in the street. He whispered the target's code name into his com, "Snake eyes, send a Jeep." He gave the coordinates. Elvis followed but broke away from Ben. Mohammed Al Safi moved through the throng of people swiftly, but Ben kept his eyes on him.

It was almost too good to be true. Mohammed Al Safi was walking right in front of them in broad daylight, alone and seemingly unaware they were stalking him. They kept their distance and watched him turn into an alley far ahead. Ben motioned to Elvis without looking at him, and he moved along parallel to the alley. Ben was now behind the target and reaching for his knife. He was so close he could smell the hookah smoke that permeated the man's clothing and skin.

Ben whispered in the com, "Take him alive."

Al Safi turned as he heard Ben speak, but Elvis surprised him by stepping in front of him. He brought him to his knees with one swift kick. Ben grabbed handcuffs from his backpack and stuffed a sweaty rag into Al Safi's mouth. As he bound his feet, Moshe's men were not far behind with the Jeep.

Tossing Al Safi inside the Jeep as it pulled into the alley, Ben grabbed a hypodermic and injected his thigh as he struggled. Ben and Elvis hopped into the Jeep as it sped away to a steel corrugated building on the edge of town, a ramshackle place in the middle of nowhere. The door opened and the Jeep slipped inside. Ben took the limp body of Al Safi and dragged him to the interrogation room, a dug basement beneath the building where the loudest screams could not be heard.

The musty odor assaulted his nostrils as they made the quick descent down the wooden ladder to the dirt below. It was claustrophobic but utilitarian. There was one light dangling from the ceiling and a steel chair beneath it. In this tomb, two rudimentary air vents were installed in the wall, one brought air in and the other sucked it out with a tiny fan. The diesel generator was the only sound in the distance behind the building. Ben quickly strapped the target into the chair and removed the cloth from his mouth. Breathing heavily, Ben drank a bottle of water as Al Safi opened his eyes. Yes, it was good to see panic in the eyes of a man who had wrought terror on many an innocent person. Now, it was his turn.

Rendition was authorized, but no records were to be kept. Ben understood what he had to do, and it could be a long involved process or a quick and dirty one. Before he decided on a strategy to garner information, he had to gauge how much this guy had to give. More than anything, he needed the location of the two terrorists who had fallen off their radar. He began with a series of questions and tried not to appear hostile, at first. He always preferred these things to go the easy way. But, if he didn't get the information he suspected the target had, he was prepared to do anything, including shooting him point blank. The fact that Al Safi lost control of his bladder during the first five minutes of questioning gave Ben a hint that this would be easy work.

At first the bastard prayed to Allah for ten minutes after pissing himself. Then the crying began.

After an hour, Ben had his fingers around his throat and was hissing in his ear in Arabic, "Tell me now, where are the others?" No answer. Ben stuffed the rag back in his mouth and took out the knife. He ran the blade along the man's neck and looked into his eyes. "You want to see Allah? I'll send you there now, you son-of-a-bitch!"

Instead of sticking the knife in his neck, Ben punched him in the gut as hard as he could. Al Safi choked on the rag and had trouble breathing. After gasping and choking for a few minutes, he nodded. Ben removed the rag. "Tell me!" he yelled for the last time in Arabic.

Descriptions and coordinates tumbled out of Al Safi's mouth in a jumble. Elvis wrote on his hand as Al Safi spoke. A green house with a balcony, names of streets, and an apartment above a bakery. But it could have been gibberish uttered to stay alive.

Ben breathed into the com, "Get someone down here with water, now! Hold him until we check out the info he gave us." Two of Moshe's men scrambled down into the tomb-like room and Ben gave them orders. "Keep him alive. We'll be back within two hours, hopefully."

Elvis wanted to run, but Ben grabbed his arm. "We can't attract attention. "The two strolled along the street using the coordinates written on Elvis' hand. The green house with the balcony was in view, just as described, about a mile north. Two men in robes were lounging on the balcony.

Ben looked at Elvis. "You're better at climbing than I am. I'll distract them for a moment and you can pull one of them inside. But, first we have to make sure no one else is inside the house. And, we have to make sure they're not armed to the teeth."

Ben spoke into the com, "Get a mosquito drone here pronto." He gave the coordinates and calmly walked by the house. He pretended to be lost and confused, peering at the addresses. Within ten minutes a young boy on a bicycle stopped next to them on the sidewalk. "Mosquito inside. Check your phone." The boy wheeled away.

Pretending to make a phone call, Ben viewed the interior of the house with the mosquito drone. No one was there at the moment. In the sweltering afternoon, the humidity had become unbearable. He glanced at Elvis, "Yup – it's time." Ben walked back toward the green house and glanced at the two men on the balcony. Speaking Spanish, he asked them for directions. While the conversation ensued, Elvis had made it up to the balcony.

The first guard was so intent on Ben, he didn't see Elvis come up from the side of the balcony. Elvis simply grabbed the guard by the back of the head and slammed it straight down into the balcony's rail. He vaulted over the guard, driving into the second one. He wrapped his arm around the other's neck in a chokehold and dragged him inside. Ben pushed through the sun-cracked wooden door in the back, and ran to the balcony. Stooping, he dragged the other man inside, hoping no one was observing.

Luckily, it was siesta and all local traffic, both pedestrian and otherwise, had come to a complete stop. Ben and Elvis quickly bound the two men. Ben spoke into his com, "Need two Jeeps at 29 Palm, pronto." Within minutes one Jeep backed up to the side door of the house and the two bound men were tossed in. Ben had injected both of them and they were dead weight for the moment.

"Good job," he said to the driver. "Now get the hell out of here. We will meet you back at the tomb." The driver of the second Jeep opened the door and Ben and Elvis scrambled in as it moved away at a rapid rate of speed.

After reviewing photographs back at the interrogation chamber, Ben realized he now had a trifecta. Al Safir, Abdullah Mizoul and Mohammed Farouk. He couldn't believe the run of luck. Three prisoners in the interrogation room was crowded, but manageable. Elvis kept them bound in uncomfortable positions. Both men spat at him when he got close enough to speak. They called him a pig and an infidel in Arabic. However, he remained calm. He'd been through this before and knew it wouldn't last long.

Tom and Gus came down to relieve them. For a brief time, Ben and Elvis raced upstairs, washed up, and ate something. Ben spoke into his com, "It's going to be a long night, guys."

An hour later, they were back in the tomb with Mizoul and Farouk. As expected, some of their swagger was gone once the stark realization had come to the terrorists they were in for a world of hurt. Like most of the men who had come to Guantanamo, they had not even been water boarded. Now they were going to long for those interrogation techniques.

Ben and Elvis took turns questioning the two new men, as Al Safir lie motionless in the corner with his hands and feet bound. After three hours of slapping the two men around, they wouldn't talk, and it was time to take the gloves off. The point being, they had said enough to Ben to give him the knowledge that they had information, but the fools actually believed they couldn't be broken. He hadn't met one yet that couldn't be.

Mizoul was kept downstairs and Farouk brought upstairs for a little while. Al Safir had passed out in the corner, but was still breathing. Mizoul knew he was in for something, but didn't know what. Ben asked him a series of questions and Mizoul refused to look at him. Tossing him onto the dirt floor, he pulled his bound hands up onto the metal chair.

"Fingers – you have ten of them – do you want to keep them?" He pulled out the fixed blade and ran it over Mizoul's index finger slowly slicing into the flesh. Blood spurted, and the tough terrorist cried out in pain. Ben stuffed the rag back into his mouth and continued cutting. Apparently, this guy wanted to play rough.

Ben stared into Mizoul's eyes. "I have PTSD, bad flashbacks of being tortured by you bastards, and a knife. I can do this all *day.*" Ben pulled the knife. The first pass was more of a yank than a cut. But, even though he'd gotten Mizoul's attention, the bastard wouldn't talk.

Mizoul screamed through the rag.

After the finger was excised, Ben took another rag out of his backpack and bound the wound to slow the bleeding. Mizoul's howling was muffled. His eyes now filled with fear, as rivulets of sweat mixed with tears poured down his face.

Ben scowled. In Arabic he shouted, "You think this is bad? Just wait. Because I'm going to keep cutting. And, once I get to your tongue, there'll be nothing left of you to talk."

Mizoul grimaced and acquiesced.

As soon as Ben removed the rag from his mouth, Mizoul blurted out everything. No longer did he hold back or put on an act filled with loyalty and pride. There was nothing left. Ben tossed him into the corner with Al Safir, and spoke into the com, "Bring down Farouk."

The men led Farouk down the wooden ladder into the tomb. He took one look at the two lying in the corner, and Ben shoved him down to the dirt floor face first. Straddling his back, Ben hissed into his ear, "Tell me."

Farouk was filled with terror. Ben took the knife and sliced off chunks of his hair. He pulled the robe off him and tossed the garment aside. Naked on the floor and trembling, Farouk cried out as Ben put the knife to his neck.

"Tell me," Ben shouted, his voice filled with rage. He saw Farouk's eyes glued to Mizoul's bloody hand. "Yes, I cut off his fingers. You're next," Ben said in Arabic. "I might cut something else off your body. You won't be needing it where you're going."

Within minutes Farouk gave him all of the information he had, and Ben even wondered if he made some of it up. There were two other detainees released earlier from Guantanamo, Ibrahim Alim Shah and Muhammed Ghafoor. The plans had been in the works for months. They were being helped by several cells in Chicago, setting up a coordinated attack in the United States, of all places. The elevated trains in Chicago would be bombed, similar to the event that occurred in Spain.

Once he got the information he called Moshe. "Tuesday is the target date. These assholes are setting up an attack in Chicago. Everything is in motion. Backpack bombs. I've got names and phone numbers. I'll text them to you. Get this shit to the FBI, CIA, and Homeland Security now!" He quickly sent the information to Moshe, then spat on the dirt floor, feeling as if he could vomit on the coward lying there trembling.

"What shall we do with the three stooges?" Elvis uttered.

Ben glanced at the men. "They're toast. Even if we keep them around and pry more out of them, would it even be worth it?" The sweat trickled down his face onto his chest. Even beneath the ground, the humidity was oppressive, sweltering. No matter how much water he consumed, he seemed to need more.

Ben ordered all of the men out of the room except the prisoners. He took a deep breath and removed the Glock19 from his shoulder holster, attaching the suppressor slowly and methodically. He noticed two of the men were already dehydrated and cowering in the corner. The third was hardly awake after the slightest roughing up. Then, another thought occurred to him.

One by one, Ben dragged the terrorists into the hole his men had dug in the basement. Their hands bound, he laid them out. It looked like one of the mass graves these men were so fond of using for their killing sprees. Except, this grave would be different in more ways than one. Ben walked away to the edge of the basement, and fingered the remote control for a garage opener.

Mizoul was the only one to look up and see the cement mixer at the edge of the space above him. His eyes widened in terror, thinking he was about to be buried in cement.

It was actually much worse.

Ben touched the remote as Mizoul took a breath to scream. Fortunately for Mizoul, that meant he took a deep, deep breath of the powdered lye that poured down onto them. Ben watched as Mizoul struggled. It was like swallowing acid. For the others, it was like swimming in it.

Murder and body disposal in one neat package. The three men ceased breathing within minutes. He spoke into the com, "Get them out of here. The flies are bad enough as it is." The men scrambled to put the bodies into bags and tossed them into the Jeep. It was black outside. A few people were milling around, but paid no attention to seven men loading stuff into a Jeep.

"Feed them to the crocodiles. There's a creek about five clicks from here, to the south." Ben exhaled. Tom nodded, "Yeah, I know where it is."

Ben dialed Moshe, "Send another Jeep for me, would you? I'm tired, bro."

Driving back to the safe house didn't feel safe. And, as if things had gone too smoothly, they were approaching what appeared to be a phony checkpoint.

"They're not police," Ben whispered into his com.

He heard Moshe's response, "Shit."

The men dressed in khakis were pointing AK's at the vehicle, and Ben had to make a quick decision. Stop and get made, or drive through taking shots, and possibly be tailed. He decided to take the latter. Either way, they'd be in a precarious situation.

Ben turned to the driver. "Run it."

The driver, who looked like a recent college graduate, didn't even look at Ben, just smiled. The vehicle roared into second, then third gear, rapidly hurtling them through the barricade. The AK's fired several bullets into the vehicle, but they were now doing sixty miles per hour zigzagging and turning down an unfamiliar road.

"Lose them," Ben ordered.

Moshe laughed. "Come now, you don't think we're that stupid, did you?" He tapped his com unit and said, "Rear car, drop the caltrops."

A medieval warfare device, the caltrops were basically a ball with four spikes coming out of it. The spikes were evenly spaced so that any way it was thrown, it still landed point up, with the other spikes acting as a tripod. It was originally used against horses and cavalry, but it worked on cars, too.

Despite losing the tail in short order, they drove for forty-five minutes, in total darkness through a rural field, then a dense jungle area. When they came upon a town, it was at least twenty miles from the inn and Ben determined it was the town of Sentini. A dot on a map, but barely that, it was slightly larger than El Chulupa. Ben observed all manner of violence taking place in the streets. Fist fights, stabbings, gun shots, drug deals, blacked out cars weaving in and out of private alleys.

"Let's get the hell out of here," Ben said, realizing they'd lost their followers. Finally, after what seemed like an eternity, they landed at the safe house. Elvis was already there taking a shower.

"Hurry up," Ben yelled to him. "I need to use the bathroom."

"All right, I'm almost done." Elvis said.

Ben stepped out into the alley to take a leak. The place reeked of urine, garbage, vomit, feces, and some smells he couldn't identify. The flies were unbearable. Babies cried. The humidity was oppressive. He didn't think he could perspire any more. His clothing was soaked with blood and sweat.

When he stepped back inside, Elvis was wrapped in a towel. "It's all yours."

Ben slapped his hand as he headed toward the shower.

Elvis looked at him, "What the hell happened to you? I thought you guys were right behind us."

Ben managed a smile, "Just another day."

He heard Elvis yell to him as he turned on the water, "Hey, Chief, if you haven't eaten, I'll get you something."

Even the water from the shower smelled like rotten eggs. But, the warm water pulsing on him washed away the grime of the day and made him feel baptized anew. Three less terrorists walked on the face of the earth, plus he got enough intel to foil an attack on American soil. Couldn't ask for more than that … except maybe four terrorists. He was satisfied with the mission. The FBI were tracking Ibrahim Alim Shah and Mohammed Ghafoor. They were doomed; a kill order had been given from the highest authority. Two more he didn't have to worry about. But, Ben would not rest until he heard they were dead, officially.

If he hadn't gone the extra mile in that interrogation, the information never would have been gleaned. The bombing of Chicago would have killed hundreds of innocent people – for what? Allah? The prophet Muhammed wanted this? What sort of sick bastard would believe this garbage? *There was nothing religious about it.* It was Nazism plain and simple. *Kill all who do not follow your sick demented leader.* It had nothing to do with God or Allah or praying or living peacefully alongside others. It was a self-centered cult, hell bent on destroying everyone and everything on the planet who didn't submit. And, it had to be stopped by unwavering men with guns who would stay up day and night, willing to do anything possible to end it.

Ben didn't need the towel to dry himself off. He let the water remain on his body. It seemed to be the only coolness he experienced for the last twenty-four hours. He slipped into a fresh shirt and cargo shorts from his backpack. Thanking Elvis for half a sandwich, he ate voraciously.

The com in his ear buzzed with the happy news that the Dark Horse Guardians had taken out twelve other targets in the course of the day, led by Randall Bettencourt. They located a gun cache with those they sought in the same building as the HUMINT group had indicated. Calmly waiting for nightfall, the men had determined their options. The G's and tiny drones helped them gain information and coordinate the strike. The dead bodies were photographed for identification, then tossed in a remote landfill, which was set afire several hours later.

The good news: all of Ben's men were intact even though they suffered bumps and bruises, cuts and sprains – they were all alive and well. Bettencourt said they hit a checkpoint, the cigarette and cash payout was generous and they were allowed through. For a moment, Ben let himself relax. He said a silent prayer of thanks as he realized God hadn't yet forsaken him.

Within minutes, his tired body dropped upon the mattress. He took Lara's shirt and inhaled her scent. How wonderful it was to close his eyes and imagine her at this moment, in this dark and revolting place. Lara, a beautiful thought to lull him to sleep. He fell into deep slumber, but it didn't last. He woke once startled by a noise outside. He instinctively reached for one of the two loaded weapons by his side. Nothing happened, but he remained awake for a while. Before sunrise he would leave in the Jeep and head back to Soto Cano.

As he lay awake he contemplated the next stop: Cuba, Leeward Point Airfield. Ben had visited Cuba when Gitmo was first populated. At the time of his visit, there were nearly 600 terrorists being held. Things were much different now. The place had changed into a terrorist country club, a joke really. It was no longer a prison-like atmosphere but one akin to a spa. Qurans were provided and handled with the utmost care. The United States didn't want to insult a terrorist. There was an exercise yard provided; tennis courts were built. The detainees were allowed to congregate. Even halal meat was served. It was astounding to him. No convenience or comfort was spared for these ruthless killers.

Sunrise came too early. Damn, he never felt so old and stiff in his life. He wanted food and good hot coffee. The Jeep ride back to Soto Cano was five hours long; thank God the driver brought breakfast. The men ate croissants and drank coffee like they'd never seen food before. When they finally got to the airport, they boarded Moshe's C130J, freshly refueled and ready for the three and a half hour flight to Cuba.

Ben reclined in the leather seat and smiled at Moshe. "A little nap would be good right about now." He closed his eyes and instantly fell asleep with the din of the team in the background excitedly talking about the coming mission in Guantanamo Bay, then Pakistan.

~ Lara ~

Rusty spent the night at Clearwater Farm with Lara and Monique. The police investigation into Officer Simpson's shooting was lengthy and detailed. Rusty's friend, John Carter, a former FBI special agent, stood watch while the others slept.

Lara's slumber was fitful. She woke to news on the radio as she dressed for the day that made her blood run cold. The Senate Intelligence Committee was about to leak classified information regarding a mission taking place in Guantanamo. Private contractors were involved. The report was being touted as the biggest intelligence leak in American history. She immediately thought of Ben. What would this mean for him if it was *his* mission being exposed? Her first response was to talk with Rusty. He had to know something about this.

Her second response to find the leaker and feed him into a wood chipper.

Not wanting to alarm Monique, Lara searched on the internet for further information. Sure enough, every news service was talking about the "leak"...the details of a CIA mission were about to be compromised. A few democrats on the Senate Intelligence Committee felt it was important for the American people to know what was being done to detainees. They claimed they were providing this information to the American people in order to be *transparent*.

What? Was this for real? She imagined it could be some sort of joke, but then realized it wasn't. She had to call Ben and let him know about the breaking news. She tapped his phone number and he answered on the second ring, "Keegan."

"Oh God, there's a Senate Intelligence Committee leak, Ben, I don't know if you've seen the news yet...but, it's not good." Lara blurted.

"Damn." She heard him mutter. "I'm not watching the news right now; how bad is it?"

Lara relayed the details to him. "Thus far the information about the report has been vague. But the story did mention contractors, roughing up terrorists." Lara whispered, "Ben, they're saying that some private contractors might be torturing terrorists. It was mentioned that their names would be exposed. What's this all about?"

"It's bullshit, that's what it is!" Ben said angrily. "I knew this was coming, but never thought they'd give out my personal information right in the middle of a covert mission. The bastards! Damn it! This puts you in the line of fire. I'm serious, Lara, if this information gets into the wrong hands, and it probably already has — there will be more than a few people wanting my head and yours, too. Look, I've got to go, darlin --- I'm sorry."

Lara's jaw clenched. This was the thanks Ben received for risking his life on every mission, doing *the government's job*? She wouldn't stand for it. She knew there was one person that Ben knew on the Senate Intelligence Committee, he was a trusted family friend and recommended him for the U.S. Naval Academy, Sam Cohen. Lara frantically found his phone number on the internet, but couldn't get through. She found a number for one of his aides and dialed it. Finally, she got a human being instead of a recording.

"I need to meet with Senator Cohen immediately," Lara said to the aide.

"And, may I ask who's calling?" the aide asked as if he'd said it a million times.

"Mrs. Ben Keegan" Lara stated flatly. "Lieutenant Ben Keegan's wife."

"One moment, please." Lara waited as she was put on hold for what seemed like an eternity.

Finally, the aide came back to the phone, "The senator can give you fifteen minutes tomorrow. But you will have to arrive in Washington and pass through security – that could take an hour or so."

"I'll be there – what time?" Lara asked.

The aide replied, "3:00 PM, that's the only free time he has left."

"I'll be there." Lara promised, and hung up.

She packed an overnight bag and drove to the train station. Rusty's friend, John Carter, was guarding as Rusty and Monique were asleep in the guest rooms. Before leaving Lara wrote a note asking Monique to take Einstein overnight, and let her know she'd be in D.C.

"Where the hell are you going?" Carter asked.

"To Washington D.C." Lara said flatly. "I have some business there. Don't say anything to Rusty until he wakes. I want him to sleep. It was a long night."

She parked the Mercedes in the train station parking lot, purchased the ticket for the capitol, and then boarded the train. Arriving early was always the best idea. She'd be sitting in Senator Cohen's outer office much earlier than he expected her. He, and everyone on the Senate Intelligence Committee, would have to look at her face all day long as they came and went to their important briefings. It was not Mr. Smith Goes to Washington, but close. She would be a one-woman army fighting against that which was pure evil: the self-centered idiots putting her homeland in grave danger, putting her husband in mortal danger, all because they wanted attention. If it was attention they wanted, she'd see that they got it. If she had to stand in front of the wall of news crews she would grant an interview explaining how leaking this report would put the lives of countless U.S. citizens in harm's way, overseas and at home. A press conference was already being set up in front of 1600 Pennsylvania Avenue. She streamed the news on her phone, anxiously watching.

Those in power had no idea who they were dealing with. She was determined to take a stand, to make a mockery of this little cabal who were hell bent on destroying her husband, a decorated war hero, the love of her life, and the future father of her children. A lioness would've paled in comparison. Lara closed her eyes and slept on the train. It was a long ride to Washington and she needed the rest. But before she closed her eyes her phone vibrated. She looked down to see Rusty's phone number.

"I know what you're doing." Rusty began. "There's really nothing we can do about this damned mess."

"Yes, there is." Lara said with determination. "Run backgrounds on the four senators. I want everything, including financials, stuff from the NSA, phone calls, I mean everything. Hack it if you have to. The leak hasn't been made public yet. I'm on my way to Washington D.C. — I plan to fight fire with fire."

There was silence on Rusty's end, then he uttered, "Listen to me, you little fool. You can't reveal your identity in front of the world. You'll put Ben's life in danger even more. Think this through. If you go before a camera, be *somebody else*...anybody else...but don't reveal your identity. I'll e-mail you everything I can get. You'd better pick up some thumb drives and a damned good disguise."

Lara smiled as the call ended. She knew there were cameras everywhere in D.C. that would be watching her every move. She pulled a scarf and sunglasses out of her backpack and slipped them on. It was imperative to keep her identity concealed. Rusty was right. She sensed there would be plenty of information to feed to the hungry news crew. And she was just the one to do the feeding. She slumped against the side of the cabin and closed her eyes from sheer exhaustion. She felt vulnerable on the train without a firearm, but knew she couldn't get through security at the senate building if she was carrying. Besides, Washington D.C. was a gun-free zone. She found this ironic, as it had one of the highest murder rates in the nation. She couldn't fight the sleep that overtook her.

Chapter 6

Guantanamo Bay, Cuba

~ Ben ~

No sooner did Ben get off the phone with Lara than Senator Cohen was on the line calling him. "I'm sorry, Chief, I couldn't stop them. I tried everything. This report is being leaked to the press by four democrats, deliberately. I'll do my best to control this, but it's already been decided."

"Uh huh. Right."

Ben knew documents would be made public with his name attached to them. This was his worst nightmare. His identity would be revealed to a whole host of terrorists who'd love to kill him and everyone in his family. He wasn't as worried about himself as he was Lara.

But he froze when he heard the Senator's next words. "And, your wife, Lara, will be here to meet with me tomorrow. I know it's about the leak and I don't know what I'm going to tell her."

"What?" Ben uttered with disbelief. "No, she'd never do such a thing and put herself in danger like that, not my wife. Are you sure it was her and not some crackpot?"

Ben heard Cohen take a deep breath and exhaled. "Yes, we traced the phone number. It was her. I have nothing to tell her, except what I've just said to you. If you can stop her, it might be a good idea. She will only make the trip to hear me say how disappointed I am with the whole mess."

Ben ran his hand over his face. "Right. I'll take care of this." He spoke to the pilot and was told the plane would be landing in ten minutes at Windward Point. From the air, he could see the coves and peninsulas along the shoreline and the ship that was moored there to spirit away the remaining detainees from Guantanamo Bay.

POTUS was planning a big press conference to announce the end of Gitmo, as if this was some meteoric accomplishment. It was all smoke and mirrors to appease his big donors and liberal constituency. It was all part of his make-believe legacy. *Ego.* That's was at the center of all evil, and the driving force behind this administration. It was sickening to watch. All Ben could do was play the role he was given.

Now that Cuba had been declared a friendly nation, the "Cactus Curtain" separating the Naval Air Base owned and operated by the United States from the Country of Cuba would still exist but it didn't carry the significance it did in earlier days. From the air, he estimated the cruise ship moored in the bay could easily house 500 people. It was an older luxury liner used now for private parties. Maintenance crews and other personnel were busy bringing provisions out to it for the long trip to the Mediterranean. The gang from Gitmo would be taking a luxury cruise to Morocco.

While still in flight, Ben dialed the phone number on the satellite phone for Captain Gooding. Gooding was an old Navy acquaintance of Ben's. He had left the Navy several years earlier than him, and worked for a cruise line as security captain. His skills were in high demand. Not only could he command a ship, he was ready, and capable of protecting the passengers as he brought along a contingent of highly trained former military personnel on all of his voyages. However, not on this one; Captain Gooding was alone. Ben spoke into the phone, "All set?"

"Yes, things are going as planned." Gooding said calmly. "Good to hear from you." The phone call ended and Ben exhaled a sigh of relief. At least *this* was going to plan, or appeared to be thus far.

As soon as the plane landed, the men entered a sequestered barracks to rest and eat. Ben, however, was on the phone trying to contact Lara. She wasn't answering her phone. It went to voicemail once. Then he called Rusty and was relieved to hear his voice, "Yeah, Chief."

Ben spoke slowly and deliberately, "Tell me this is some sort of joke...Lara on a train to Washington D.C. to see Senator Cohen?"

Ben sensed Rusty didn't want to tell him what he said next, "No, Chief. She's going. And, I'm helping her. She will be in disguise. I've got the stuff she requested all e-mailed to her. She's downloading it on a zip drive right now. I thought she was crazy at first, too. But, now I'm not so sure. I think she's smarter than all of us."

"Are you serious?" Ben closed his eyes to stifle the anger rising in him. "What the hell is she going to do? There's no stopping this clown show. They have an agenda."

"The information I sent to Lara just might stop them." Rusty chuckled. "Scandals, dirt, yes. That's the stuff we need right now, and these four idiots have plenty of it in their past. Hell some of it is present. I'm talking about possible felony charges, sex with underage girls, gun-running. The works. The press will eat this stuff up. It's our only leverage and we have to use it."

Ben couldn't believe he was hearing this correctly. "So, you and Lara have teamed up and will be in front of the press at the White House to release all of this?"

Rusty corrected him, "Not exactly. She will meet with Senator Cohen first and give the information to him. He will call an emergency meeting with the four senators and let them know what will happen if the intel is leaked. They will have only one chance to destroy the report and pull back the rhetoric. Actually, they will be asked to resign by the Senate Majority Leader. It will only be a matter of time before these scandals emerge. Lara and I uncovered a volcano waiting to erupt. Lara wanted leverage, and she's got it."

Ben couldn't believe what he was hearing, but also knew he couldn't stop her, even if he did get Lara on the phone. She was on a mission to protect him, even if it meant endangering her own life. He hoped to God she wasn't in D.C. without a concealed weapon. But he knew she'd probably abide by the laws of the district and go without it. His focus should be on the Guantanamo mission, but now his mind was on Lara. He had to trust she would be all right. He feared for her safety more than he did any situation he might encounter.

If he remained pissed off and frustrated, he wouldn't get anywhere with this mission. He had to focus and concentrate on the task at hand. He trusted Rusty and Lara, and hoped to God they could pull off a miracle. The plane was banking and coming in for a landing. He sat down and put the seatbelt on, still deep in thought and closed his eyes.

Gus slapped him on the back. "Worried, Chief?"

"Nah, just thinking." Ben managed a smile. "We got this."

Washington D. C.

~ Lara ~

A group of satellite trucks had set up shop in front of the White House long before Lara arrived. Her first stop was to a hair salon, where she purchased a long blonde number along with plenty of make-up. She wrapped her head in the scarf and kept dark glasses on while in the store so the security camera would not get a good image. She made sure to turn away from the cameras, at least the ones that were visible. She entered the train station restroom, not the safest place in the world.

No sooner did she get in the stall than she heard another person enter; then the voice of a man. "Pssst, come here, Lara, it's me."

As she opened the stall door, she saw Rusty beckoning to her in the handicapped stall, waving her in. She got into the space with him and closed the door. Whispering and suppressing a wry little smile, Rusty helped her transform into someone else. With the blonde wig, make-up and jewelry, she began to look like one of the Channel 5 news anchors. Rusty kept his chuckling to a minimum, although she could see he was holding his breath. The door to the ladies room opened and closed. Women came and left in rapid succession, toilets flushing. No one needed the handicapped stall, thank goodness. Rusty finally spoke, "I'll exit first and will hang around outside. Wait a few minutes and walk out of here toward your destination. I'm your bodyguard."

Lara did as he instructed. It was a better plan than she could have imagined. But then, he was a former FBI agent and knew every trick in the book, and probably invented some. She strutted through the train station as people stared at her with their mouths open. She was being mistaken for someone else, someone famous. Whom, she didn't know. But her disguise was good enough to make the people at the train station point and stare. She felt ready for prime time.

As Lara entered the side door of the guard shack outside of the senate building, she knew she was passing through the first layer of security. A female secret service employee went through her backpack and searched her bodily, then she was escorted to another area where she sat and waited. Another female in uniform brought her into a small room. "What is your business here today, Miss Rivera?" Lara had almost forgotten that Rusty had given her a forged identity.

Lara spoke with a Spanish accent, "I'm here to see Senator Cohen. He is expecting me. Please give him the message that I am here early. My appointment was at 3:00, but he said to call him as soon as I arrive."

Lara was lying through her teeth, hoping beyond hope that Senator Cohen would know it was her.

The uniformed woman made the call to the senator's office, exchanged a few words, then she hung up the phone. "I'll escort you up, Miss Rivera." The congress building was filled with people coming and going. She imagined many of them were lobbyists with offices nearby for convenience. She recognized many of the politicians, as she passed them on the staircase or in the hallway. She garnered a few stares, but for the most part, no one took great interest in her. The people she encountered seemed to be wrapped up in their own little worlds, hurrying to attend a meeting somewhere.

She was left in the outer office of Senator Cohen where his staff resided. "She's the one I called you about," the female officer said as she departed. "Have a nice day, Miss Rivera." The door closed and locked. Lara smiled at the woman behind the desk, a middle-aged lady with her dark hair secured in a bun that looked too tight. She peered over her glasses at Lara, "Miss Rivera?"

Lara nodded, "Yes, I am early, but let Senator Cohen know I have important information for him. It will only take a minute of his time." The dark-haired woman disappeared, while two men in the far corner of the office were eyeing her and whispering to one another. Lara imagined they were mistaking her for someone else.

As soon as the dark-haired woman appeared, she waved Lara toward her. "Come along, Senator Cohen has invited you in, but please be aware you have only a few minutes. He is due to attend an important senate intelligence meeting." Lara knew the information she was going to give him could change everything in that meeting.

Senator Cohen was sitting at his desk when she entered his office, but he stood and dismissed the dark-haired woman. Once the door was closed, he whispered, "Lara?"

She removed the glasses and winked at him, "Yes, it's me. But I'm undercover. You understand why, I'm sure." She handed him the flash drive. "Preview this right now before you go into that meeting. It's my reason for being here."

The senator moved to his desk and viewed the contents of the drive. "Holy Jesus!" was all that escaped from his lips. Once he recovered from the shock, he managed to ask her, "Where did you get all of this?"

Lara peered at him over her glasses. "Don't ask questions. It's all legitimate. Use it as leverage against the four senators threatening to leak the information that will kill my husband and thousands of other innocent people serving this country."

The senator printed off the material and pressed a button. The dark-haired woman appeared. "Make four copies of this, immediately. It's classified." The dark-haired woman glanced at Lara, but hastily took the paperwork to the locked copy room off the senator's office.

"By God, Lara, I think I can do this." He muttered as she watched beads of sweat forming on his upper lip. "I just hope it works."

"It will work." Lara assured him. "Their egos are all that matters. But they'll go down in a short time in flames. Once the senate leadership reads this, they will be asked to step down. The ties to the sex trafficking group and the drug dealers will sink them. They should be more careful who they accept money from. The intelligence report will be destroyed by then. You will make a few more enemies, but in the long run, you're doing the right thing."

As she was escorted out of the building, Lara hoped that Senator Cohen would have the gumption to go forward with the leverage he now held in the palm of his hand. He seemed like a man of his word. There was something about him that made Lara want to trust him. She saw Rusty out of the corner of her eye as she got back to the street in front of the White House. The news services had multiplied out front. There were food vendors feeding the crews, as lights and cameras were being set up.

When Lara walked up to one of the rookie reporters, she asked, "I'm just curious – what's going on here?"

The reporter was young, probably twenty-something, and right out of college, "You haven't heard? There's a showdown going on in the Senate Intelligence Committee. Big news. We are here to get it first." The reporter was called away for a moment, then he returned. His brown eyes lit up, "We just got a call from Senator Cohen's office...he's going to make a statement in an hour! Hot damn!"

Lara turned and walked away with Rusty close behind. She got onto the Amtrak train and Rusty got on the same car but sat a few seats behind her. She sent a text to him on her phone, *Thanks*. He sent a text back to her, *You're welcome*. As the train pulled out of Washington D.C., Lara felt her body go limp with relief. A few minutes later, Rusty walked down to the seat next to Lara. "Is this seat taken, Miss?" he asked politely.

"No, it's all yours." She said without looking up from her magazine. Lara felt his arm against hers and her foot touched his. He pulled his cap down over his eyes and slumped into his snoozing position. But he wasn't sleeping. He whispered, "You did it, kid. I just saw the news on my phone."

Lara whispered back, "No, *we* did it."

Guantanamo Bay, Cuba

~ Ben ~

The sky was pink and gold as the sun slipped below the horizon in Guantanamo Bay. It was a lovely sight to witness. It was no more than a signal for Ben.

There were few lights on the deserted bay where the cruise ship was anchored, and Ben put on the swim fins and goggles and slipped beneath the warm ocean water. His face and neck were blackened with resin and he swam underwater without making a ripple. He took his time getting out to the ship. Everything had to be done correctly with precision. No hurrying. He preferred not to use the breather. He loved swimming long distances beneath the surface. He touched his keeper making sure the mines were in place on his chest.

Once he was alongside the vessel, the only sound was his breathing and the water lapping against the hull. He removed two magnetic devices and carefully attached them to the hull, one on the stern and one near the engine room centerboard. He climbed the stern ladder and moved around the deck strategically placing C4 devices in places they'd not be seen. Underneath the stern rail was perfect. Ten in all. The electronics were set.

He climbed back down the ladder and slipped into the water. There was no wind. In the darkness, a mosquito buzzed around his head momentarily but he made no movement. Once finished with his task, he silently slinked beneath the water and swam in a southerly direction parallel to the shore. There was a large rock in the shallow water that would hide him as he emerged.

As a Navy SEAL, underwater demolition was his passion. Although he was a skilled sniper and gifted in hand-to-hand combat, this was his true love. The quiet nighttime solitude of the ocean was like a tonic for his weary soul. He dipped beneath the surface and swam underwater until he got to the shallow edge. He pulled himself onto the wet sand and remained motionless for a moment near the rock. No one was around. The guards far away on the point had knowledge of his mission, but they didn't know his identity. They'd been briefed hours before he landed.

He removed his fins, slipped on water shoes, and made his way back to the barracks. Tired and hungry, he ate in the mess hall kitchen alone. Moments later, Moshe caught up to him. "How'd it go?"

Ben smiled. "All set."

"Good." Moshe slapped him on the back. "Have you called the Coast Guard yet?"

"That's my next task." Ben said, "Right after I finish eating."

The men were in the conference room with Moshe. Alone and quiet, Ben sprawled upon his bunk and tapped his phone. "Captain Becker? It's your favorite person."

The man on the other end of the phone laughed as he recognized Ben's introduction. An old roommate from the Naval Academy, Becker was one of Ben's best friends and was running a Coast Guard cutter between Florida and Cuba.

"What's the deal?" Becker asked. "The commander mentioned you'd be calling. I figured whatever you had going on would be nothing but trouble."

"It's a boat by the name of The Fiesta, an older cruise ship. You know the cargo they're carrying. It's precious cargo, according to the government anyway. You will need to stop the vessel and board it. But, you need to get Captain Gooding *off* that boat long enough for me to do my thing. And, for God's sake, make sure you are far enough away. And, somehow get the five crew members off there. I want them taken away, simultaneously."

"Sure thing, Chief." Becker replied. "Don't worry. I've got an idea that's sure to work."

"Whatever it is, just make sure Captain Gooding and the crew are off that ship. You remember the signal, right?" Ben asked.

"Got it." Becker responded and hung up.

Exhaling, Ben leaned back in his chair. The kitchen was quiet and he enjoyed the solitude for a moment longer. He knew he should join the team in the war room to go over the finer points of the mission in

Pakistan. It was déjà vu really – he'd be hunting the same bastards he had put into Guantanamo Bay detention seven years ago. He thought of Sam and Javier. They'd given their lives for this shit. At moments like this, he understood with great clarity why veterans returning from Iraq and Afghanistan were suffering from depression and committing suicide. All that they had accomplished, given life and limb for, was being systematically dismantled before their eyes.

Monique and Einstein were both asleep on the sofa when Lara got home that night. Two police detectives greeted her at the top of the driveway. "Just keeping watch, ma'am."

The two men told her to sleep well. Yeah, right.

Although Lara had slept on the train, she was exhausted. The dog stirred as she entered the kitchen and he whined with delight to see her.

Monique turned off the television. "So, how was your trip?"

"Fruitful," Lara smiled. "Thanks for staying with the dog. Please stay the night; I think it would be a good idea, seeing as we have Aaron and Tim stalking us."

Monique eyed her suspiciously, "Lara, exactly what's going on?"

"There's a bit of a problem." Lara knew she had to tell Monique but wrestled with the words she'd use. "We need to stay safe. Those guys following us….they're connected with terrorists. They know I am Ben's wife."

Monique's demeanor changed. "You aren't kidding. Oh God, Lara. What are we going to do?"

"Nothing." Lara said flatly. "I'm going to take Einstein out for his after-dinner walk, a very short one along the beach, then back to the house."

Monique stared at her, "I'll come with you. I've been inside all day. Is it safe?"

"The detectives outside are monitoring the security feed. It's sophisticated and covers the entire perimeter of the property. Plus, they're armed. I'm carrying, too. We do have to be cautious. Hold on, I want to change. I'll be right back." Lara walked down the hallway to the master bedroom searching momentarily for her sweatshirt and pants.

Once in the quiet solitude of the room that reminded her most of Ben, she exhaled. Her energy was flagging but she wanted to go for the walk to clear her head. She so wished Hawk was there to talk with her. He always knew the right thing to say when she was filled with anxiety. But she was buoyed by Monique's companionship. Securing her holster and Glock, she slipped into yoga pants, a sweatshirt and sneakers. Bounding into the kitchen, Lara glanced down at the ancient book of Shakespearean sonnets, paused, and couldn't resist touching it lightly with her finger.

"Where did that come from?" Monique asked. "It looks like an antique first edition."

"A good friend gave it to me," Lara whispered. "Sometimes I touch it for good luck." Lara noticed Monique was ready with the dog and she tapped the security code after putting on a fleece jacket. The two walked out. Lara's sidearm was snugly resting on her hip. She fingered it relishing the feeling of safety it imbued.

"Do you always carry that thing?" Monique asked nodding toward the 9mm Glock19 hidden beneath Lara's sweatshirt.

"Yes, why?" Lara replied.

"I was thinking of getting my permit to carry...you know?" Monique's voice drifted off.

Lara smiled. "I know just the guy to help you out."

Walking Einstein along the beach seemed to center her once again, and Lara felt she was home in the safety of Clearwater Farm. Returning minutes later she caught sight of the officers at the top of the driveway.

Monique nodded toward them. "So, these two are our bodyguards?"

Lara smiled. "Yes. I'm glad they're here, actually. I'm exhausted and will rest a bit easier with two seasoned detectives. Not to change the subject, but we have lots of work to do tomorrow. We have a few clients who need design work done. Are you ready to put yourself through the grinder?"

Monique smiled for the first time in what seemed like days. "Yes, I'd like to sink my teeth into a project. What's on the agenda?"

Lara rattled off the latest projects and Monique was focused on the details of the work they had before them.

This was good. Monique was gaining her footing. Bettencourt was gone, but she had accepted that he would return. She was hopeful. That's all they both clung to for the moment: hope.

The next morning, tailed by police officers, both women had breakfast at the diner and unlocked the bungalow, ready to tackle the latest projects. The moment Lara unlatched the bungalow door thoughts of Hawk overwhelmed her. She inhaled deeply and moved to the closet to hang her coat next to the denim work jacket she coveted. Her fingers touched the fabric briefly.

"You okay?" Monique asked.

"Yes. I'll hang your jacket for you." Lara forced a little smile and slipped Monique's jacket onto a hanger next to hers. She closed the wooden door, and the two sat in the living room while they sorted through the details of each task.

"Do you want the Robinson project?" Lara asked Monique.

"Sure. That's the renovation of a massive library and living room. The one with the beautiful fireplace, right?" Monique asked.

"Yes. Good for you to tackle. Don't hesitate to ask for help. I wanted the Hoffman job. Oh look, they have three children. I'll be designing their bedrooms. That will be fun!" Lara whispered.

After a few minutes, Monique collected her materials and moved into the tiny side office to make phone calls. Lara moved into the other bedroom, now an office, the one where Hawk had been sleeping when he was there. She tried to not think about him for the time being. There were many days she had sat on the sleeper sofa in this room and sobbed, unable to stop herself. But now she turned her attention to the needs of three young children and the Hoffman family.

The oldest Hoffman child was ten years old, her name was Rebecca. Then there was Samuel, he was seven. And, Jonathan was only five. Jonathan. That was Ben's father's name. She liked the sound of it and imagined if they ever had a baby boy, it would be one of the names she'd choose. For a second her hand ran over her abdomen and she imagined what it would be like to be pregnant with Ben's baby. She knew he wanted children, but they'd never really had a lengthy, detailed discussion about it. Her greatest fear was raising a child alone. She pushed the thought out of her mind and concentrated on this Jonathan before her. She studied the photos of the existing room the client had sent along with a photo of the child. He had dark hair and blue eyes. Oh God. Little Jonathan Hoffman was adorable and he reminded her of Ben.

Immersing herself in the project, she called Mrs. Hoffman and scheduled an initial appointment, then called the usual contractors to see what their schedules were like. The two detectives were sitting on the porch of the bungalow. They were kind enough to ask what Monique and Lara wanted for lunch. A delivery from the deli arrived. They worked all day, as if everything was normal, but it wasn't. Lara kept waiting for the Mustang to reappear, or to turn around and see Aaron or Tim. Even though the detectives were hanging around, she felt uneasy but didn't let Monique know.

Chapter 7

Guantanamo Bay, Cuba

~ Ben ~

The cruise ship was scheduled to leave Guantanamo Bay Cuba at 8:00 AM. It was sunny and warm with calm seas. Ben imagined Lara was home now, probably preparing to take Einstein for his morning beach walk then head into the office.

Ben had watched the sun as it rose, painting the sky a pale shade of pink, then gold. On a computer screen he focused on Captain Gooding as he expertly moved the cruise ship away from its mooring. Fifty miles out he would cut the engines and make a call to the Coast Guard for assistance. Ben watched and waited patiently as he tracked the ship on the computer screen. The GPS coordinates were fed to him via a geo-synchronous satellite that was accurate within several inches. Two cooks and three stewards were aboard with 132 terrorists-cargo...Ben didn't like to think of them as passengers. These bastards would not be returning to the battlefield. They were on his turf now.

The text to Becker was sent as the ship cruised to the exact longitude and latitude Ben had planned. He heard Captain Gooding's call for help to the Coast Guard Cutter, Reliance.

"Mayday-Mayday-Mayday, This is The Fiesta, 50 nautical miles northeast of Guantanamo Bay Cuba. Six crew, 132 passengers. Engine problems. Possible tow. Can remain afloat but no steerage. Engine room alarm sounding. Description of our vessel: The Fiesta is a 500 meter cruise ship with special mission. Over."

Ben listened as Captain Becker responded. "Fiesta, this is the U.S. Coast Guard Reliance. We are approximately 25 nautical miles away due west. Do you copy?"

Captain's Gooding's call for help was answered and now Ben would wait as the Coast Guard approached the vessel. Moshe walked into the room and broke the tension. "How's it going?"

"According to plan, so far." Ben didn't move. "I just hope this goes smoothly. Plan B is not the option I want to go with.

"You mean boarding the vessel and taking it?" Moshe asked.

"Yes, they're SEALs, and they'd make pretty good pirates, but I don't want my men put into that situation. It's important this goes the way I originally planned." Ben exhaled. He didn't realize he had been breathing shallowly. "Would you be a good soldier and get me a coffee?"

Moshe left the room and came back with the coffee, in a giant plastic cup just the way Ben liked it, fresh, strong and black, borderline espresso. Captain Becker wore a communication device and Ben could hear the conversation. Finally, after what seemed like hours, Becker pulled alongside the disabled Fiesta and asked Captain Gooding to board the Coast Guard vessel. Ben listened to the conversation as the Coast Guard Captain asked for paperwork, and then pretended to call a towing company.

Meanwhile, one of the Coast Guard ensigns boarded the Fiesta, and the crew lined up providing their paperwork. The ensign acted like something was amiss with the paperwork. The five crew members were marched onto the U.S. Coast Guard vessel Reliance for further scrutiny. Within minutes, Ben heard the roar of the motors. He watched the Reliance on the computer screen as it pulled away at a good rate of speed. He inhaled and waited as the longitude and latitude of the Reliance made its mark. It was at that moment he dialed a phone number. The first ring set off the explosive devices attached to the bottom of the Fiesta. The second ring set off the C4 devices placed above the waterline.

The new generation C4 was incredibly powerful, nearly ninety percent explosive, with twice the crushing power of dynamite. The 500-foot vessel exploded. A minute passed.

Captain Becker on the *Reliance* keyed his microphone and said simply uttered, "Holy shit, she's gone." It wasn't until that moment that Ben allowed himself to exhale a deep sigh of relief.

Although the explosion was fifty miles offshore, he witnessed the first wisps of black smoke on the horizon. He knew the explosion blew the vessel into splinters of fiberglass, the diesel fuel caught fire and floated atop the ocean water. The bodies would be blown to bits. Pieces and parts of the ship had shattered and embedded into them. If anyone lived through that impact, they're odds of survival would be a few minutes, but most would perish immediately upon detonation. There would be body parts floating in the ocean. The sharks would have a feeding frenzy long before anyone could get to the vessel or figure out what had happened.

Moshe walked back inside the room. Ben smiled at him, "We've got a plane to pack. When the Dark Horse guys come back in, we need to move."

"All is well. I can tell by your smile." Moshe responded.

"One hundred and thirty-two less..." Ben said flatly. "But we have miles to go before we sleep."

The C-130J was refueled and already being packed for the long trip back to the Middle East, first to Israel, then Pakistan, where Ben couldn't wait to sink his teeth into the last leg of the mission. He was elated the flight would last fourteen hours. This meant he could sleep — really sleep — and he pulled Lara's shirt out of his backpack and reclined the seat fully. After drinking a bottle of spring water, he laid on his side and bunched Lara's shirt up for a pillow. For a moment he thought about how crazy his life was. *The rules of the games he played kept changing.* In his world nothing was stable, except Lara. She was the one constant he could be sure of. Willfully, he succumbed to the sleep that overtook him, inhaling the scent of his wife, missing her more than ever.

Eight hours later, he woke to the sound of the landing gear clicking and the jet engines throttling back. Refueling in Bermuda, the men stepped off the plane but remained on the tarmac as fresh food was delivered. Within an hour, they were wheels up destined for Israel. From there, the team would travel to Pakistan, one of the places Ben seemed drawn to like a magnet. As miserable a place as it was, it did have its appeal: the whole country was akin to a huge tenement filled with rats and his task was to rid it of vermin in a systematic manner.

Thank goodness decent food was delivered to the plane during the refueling. A steward brought him a tray with fresh vegetables and chicken. Not the frozen stuff. This was the real thing. He ate hungrily, and noted the silence on the plane as the team did the same. He'd lost at least five pounds since he started this journey. He knew the food in Pakistan would be putrid. They'd load up with protein snacks and MRE's at the base in Israel.

Returning home to Clearwater Farm with her protectors in tow, Lara began feeling the oppression of being watched, not so much by the detectives as the two in the Mustang. She dialed the police station and spoke to Captain Redman, the man in charge of the case.

"I was just going to call you, Mrs. Keegan," Redman sounded surprised.

"What's up?" Lara asked.

"We know more about Aaron Brown and Tim Crosby. They are college students at the university where your husband teaches. These two originally lived in New York City before coming to Portland. Our counter-terrorism connections with the NYPD gave us a massive of information about them. Would you mind if I stopped by to go over a few things with you?"

"That would be fine. I'll be here." Lara ended the call while many thoughts swirled through her mind. It couldn't be good news if the captain of special investigations was dropping by personally."

Monique was in the kitchen making a salad. "Why the sad face?"

Lara didn't know what to say. "We'll be having a visitor in a few minutes...Captain Redman. He has some information he wants to give us, but wanted to talk with us in person."

"Oh, that can't be good." Monique's brows knit together with concern.

"No. I was thinking the same." Lara stared into space.

When Redman arrived, his car whisked down the long driveway. With a bounce in his step he approached the porch door. Lara greeted him, "Hello, come in."

He removed his coat and Lara took it for him. *Damn, if he's taking off his coat, this was probably going to be a long drawn out conversation.* "Can I get you a coffee or something to drink?"

He was a medium-sized man, with a muscled build beneath the suit. The permanent furrow in his brow made her think he was probably forty years old, with a wife, kids and a mortgage. Lots on his mind. He wore glasses and had the appearance of Clark Kent, minus the superman shirt. He sat at the table in the kitchen with Lara serving coffee. Monique joined them.

"Lovely old place you have here." Redman started out smiling. He was trying to be nice, because he probably had something earthshattering to tell them.

Monique was staring at him, as if waiting for the words to tumble out of his mouth.

"Thank you," Lara responded. "What information are you going to give us?"

Captain Redman's face changed to a solemn stare. He removed his glasses and closed his eyes for a moment before putting them back on. His dark eyes met hers as if he was trying to gauge her reaction before he spoke. "I don't want to alarm you, but there's been an intelligence leak in Washington...your husband's name has been given to some very bad people...terrorists, actually."

"So, that's why Aaron Brown and Tim Crosby are following us?" Lara shot back.

"Yes. They've been contacted by someone in Pakistan. Brown and Crosby are college students, but they're part of a sleeper cell here in the United States, ready, willing and able to do the bidding of someone wielding a lot of power and money." Redman exhaled as if that was only part one of the bad news.

"There's more...." Lara prompted him.

"Yes. The mission your husband is on has been compromised. The targets he is hunting have been tipped off. They know he is coming for them and the most likely scenario is not good." Redman could barely get the words out.

"What's the likely scenario?" Lara leaned forward and stared into his eyes.

"These men...the ones your husband is hunting down...they may be hunting him." Redman closed his eyes after saying the words and swallowed hard. He removed his glasses once more and set them on the table. "Please, understand, we are doing everything in our power right now to communicate with your husband and the others working with him. But of utmost importance, we have reason to believe the terrorists know *your* name, know that you're his wife, and you have become a valuable possession to them right now. We need to keep you safe."

Lara felt the wave of nausea hit her before the rage began. "Who leaked this information? I want to know!"

"I don't know." Captain Redman tried to calm her by touching her hand on the table. "Look, we --- I'm doing everything possible. Please understand..."

Whatever he said after that was a moot point, as far as Lara was concerned. Ben was in danger. She was in danger. Monique was in danger. And the only feeling flooding Lara's veins was pure rage.

It was as if Captain Redman read her mind. "And, don't call anyone and tell them about this. The less people involved, the better."

"Tell me this," Lara posited. "Is the FBI involved in this? The CIA? The Special Activities Director? Is the executive office at the white house aware?"

Redman looked away. "All of the people who *need* to be involved already know about this, Mrs. Keegan. Trust me. We are doing all that we can."

Lara never felt comfortable with anyone who said the words "trust me." And, she certainly did not feel any sense of security at this moment. Berating Redman wasn't going to get her anywhere, this much she knew. She thanked him for coming, and for the round-the-clock protection and sent him on his way. As she watched his vehicle leave the driveway, she knew in her heart, that she'd need to defend herself, and Monique would need to learn how to shoot a gun in a short period of time.

She picked up her cell phone and dialed the one man she always knew she could count on.

Chapter 8

Pakistan

~ Ben ~

Pakistan during rainy season was every bit as charming as Pakistan during dry season. As the armored Humvees made their way toward the border, Ben was painfully aware that insertion was the most dangerous aspect of the mission. According to statistics, most missions were aborted before they got underway due to detection by the enemy. Dressed as Pakistanis, Moshe's unit and Ben's team blended into the landscape. If stopped they had plenty of cigarettes and money to pass out to the corrupt government officials and all of the men spoke the dialect of the region.

The danger was being stopped by those they were chasing. If made, they'd be taken captive, tortured and killed. Not a cheerful scenario to ponder, but the thought kept the team hyper-vigilant. Strict attention was paid attention to every detail of their surroundings. Several drones followed their movements, and F4 Phantoms were ready to scramble from Israel within a moment's notice. But none of these things made Ben feel totally confident. When you came right down to it, nothing ever did.

The American people were being lied to on a daily basis by those in power. However, there was a delicate balance. Those at the top didn't want to cause panic, create hysteria, get those 300 million guns out there locked and loaded. The U.S. government feared the gun-toting patriotic, second amendment lovers more than they did radical terrorists – go figure. *And, there were times when Ben actually wondered which side his own government was on.*

At the very top levels, there existed an inexplicable bond with the Muslims attacking the United States and everything it stood for. Yet there was no will to go after these enemies of the state on the battlefield. *Why?* The president was actually talking to Iran about nuclear weapons and crafting an agreement that would allow them to build one. There were a far too many Islamists serving in high positions in the very agencies tasked with keeping the country safe. Had the fox been in the hen house for so long, the hens were afraid to even make a sound? Or, was the commander-in-chief's ego so big he wanted to be known for shutting down all defense of Iraq, Afghanistan, shuttering Guantanamo, Bagram, and letting every terrorist go? Hell, next on his agenda would be to open all of the prisons in the United States and unleash a torrent of crime the likes that had never been seen. That would fundamentally change America. *It would destroy it.*

This was either ego-maniacal leadership or blind stupidity; what's worse, it could be both. It didn't matter what name you gave it. What mattered, was how the United States of America, the greatest country in the history of mankind, was being taken apart brick by brick. Laws were being broken at the highest levels. The constitution of the greatest country in the world was being trampled upon. There was no doubt any longer. Four star generals at the Pentagon were boldly speaking out publically about the actions being taken at the top. *And no one could stop it. To say this was frustrating would be an understatement. But for Lieutenant Ben Keegan, these actions were undermining his cause, his reason to exist.*

Ben focused on killing those he was being paid to eliminate. The list was long. Guantanamo *detainees* was such a nice way to describe these butchers in the comfort of a congressional meeting room. But Ben knew *what* they really were, *who* they really were. To call them animals would insult animals, for animals paired off in the beauty of the natural world and nurtured their young. Animals didn't kill their own, rape them and burn them to death. They didn't subjugate other animals to slavery. Animals didn't plot and plan to destroy the earth and all who disagreed with them.

No. The men he was hunting were no longer human and they didn't deserve to be labeled animals; they'd morphed into satanic demons. That's why pulling the trigger, putting the bullet through their skulls, left him cold. There would be no fist-bumps or selfies after the killing was done. He'd leave that to the oval office. Lieutenant Ben Keegan didn't have his ego in the game; only his head was in this game, because this was being played for the highest stakes. As far as he was concerned, losing was not an option.

Recent Guantanamo prisoners released had scattered across the Pakistani landscape like the cockroaches that they were. They thought they were hidden, but he knew their locations. The biggest catch of all would be Salib Madi. Ben wanted to take him alive, if possible, for rendition.

The normally temperate weather was much cooler than usual. The unrelenting rain delayed their arrival to the first stop, the city of Khost in Afghanistan, bordering Pakistan. Disguised as Punjab Pakistanis, the team took the up-armored Humvees over the highway at a reduced rate of speed due to the heavy rain. Shit. He hated rain. Besides interfering with safe travel, the mud it created sometimes gave too much away when it came to footprints and tire marks. But the driving rain today was unrelenting, causing flooding, washing everything away, even parts of roads.

To make matters worse, Moshe's vehicle broke down half way to Dera Ghazi Khan.

"Damn," Moshe muttered into his com. "We've got a flat. Got to pull into Bhakkar. One of my guys knows the area. Can you drift into the market area down the street from where I'll stop?"

"No problem. Let me know when you're back on the road." Ben uttered, feeling a sense of dread. "Damn, I hate it when unexpected shit happens."

Elvis gave him a sidelong glance. "You think this is trouble?"

"Yup." Ben grimaced as he continued past Moshe's vehicle. "He's got a flat. I don't know why he's pulling into Bhakkar. I hate Bhakkar."

Moshe was back on the com, "Hey, I heard that. Bhakkar is where we are stopping. We know a garage there, it's a friendly. We can change the two flats we have and get some extra tires and be on our way. I don't want this caravan to be seen along the side of the road...it's too obvious."

Elvis smiled as Ben rolled his eyes. "Shit, I could have those two flats changed in about ten minutes on the side of the road. I hate detours. You know that."

"Head to the center of Bhakkar. Wait to hear from me. There's something else going on, too." Moshe said his voice tinged with concern. Ben suddenly realized this was more than just a flat tire. Moshe wanted to deviate from their original course. But why? He did as he was told and blew past Moshe. Then, Ben turned around and slowed down. Backtracking, he approached the center of Bhakkar, a short distance away from the garage Moshe pulled into. Parking on the side of the road in darkness, he slumped against the door of the vehicle ready for a short snooze if Elvis would stay awake to watch.

"Damn, I hate this time-wasting shit." Ben muttered.

~ Abdul Rahman Shafir ~

Abdul could not see well in the driving rain, but perched upon the roof of a building along the highway, he thought he saw the caravan he was expecting. Ten Humvees of varying colors passed by. They did not all come at one time. There were two or three at a time. They were exactly what he'd expect Keegan to be using.

He spoke Punjabi into his phone. "It's them, I think."

It was his good fortune that in the intelligence document, the United States had given the parameters of this mission, and he now had faces to put with the names of the infidels. If he killed or captured Lieutenant Ben Keegan, he'd be given a half-million dollar bounty. But better than that, he'd gain status in the Islamic organization. The entire twenty-five years of his life, Abdul had lived for a moment like this.

However, Abdul knew he was in a precarious position. Killing Keegan would be much easier than capturing him. First he'd have to conquer the fear that rippled through him every time he thought about the man. Keegan's reputation preceded him. More Humvees whizzed by heading in the general direction of Dera Ghazi Khan where Ibrahim Ismail waited. Abdul followed in the red Subaru. One of the vehicles had stopped by the side of the road and a dark haired man jumped out and checked the tires. The loosely held convoy continued on, but two Humvees pulled off to enter the center of Bhakkar, deviating from the course.

This was unexpected. Abdul had to make a decision quickly, so he followed the disabled Humvee for two miles and watched it enter a garage. Abdul followed closely, but drove past those he followed as they pulled into the car repair facility. He drove by following the other vehicle into the center of Bhakkar and watched it park. The vehicle just sat there on the side of the street with the occupants inside. They were a short distance from the repair facility, as if they were watching, waiting.

The markets and streets were quiet in the black rain-soaked night. The car repair business was closed, so Abdul couldn't figure out why the men stopped there. Maybe they had plans to steal something, or there was something else going on. He coasted up the street and turned around, finally parking underneath the shadow of a large overhang from an adjacent building. From his vantage point, he could see the parked vehicle with the two men inside, and he was at an angle so he could view the Humvee if it pulled out of the facility. He stared in that general direction for what seemed like an hour.

In Punjabi he whispered on his phone to Ibrahim, "Two of them have stopped in Bhakkar. I don't know where the others are. They may have continued on to Dera Ghazi Khan."

"Stupid shithead." Ibrahim hissed at him on the phone. "You lost Keegan? Or, is he in the vehicles you are following?"

"It's too dark to know who is in which vehicle. But it is definitely them. There are ten Humvees. Eight of them are out there somewhere. They continued on the highway as these two pulled off. What did you expect me to do?" Abdul felt his hackles rise. He felt as if someone was watching him.

After hanging up with Ibramin, Abdul felt an eerie feeling alone in the dark. The car engine was silent and the only sound was the rain pelting on the metal roof he'd parked beneath. Visibility was almost zero, as an intense burst of rainfall pummeled the overhang and droplets bounced off the ground with force. Something about the garage down the street silently forbade him to drive by again. He watched the minutes tick by on the dashboard clock. Sixty-two minutes, and the rain wasn't letting up. Ibrahim's voice was impatient as he answered the vibrating phone. "What are you doing?"

"Watching the garage. They're inside. It's been more than an hour," Abdul said flatly.

Chapter 8

Pakistan

~ Ben ~

Ben had peeled off right after Moshe's Humvee took the off-ramp. Elvis noticed the Subaru following them miles ago. The ten Humvees planned a rendezvous point as two split off at the market in Bhakkar. Ben decided to do a little reconnaissance around the garage where Moshe's Humvee was safely sheltered for the time being. That's when he spied it. The Subaru. Sitting beneath the overhang of a building, it appeared the vehicle was empty.

Moshe's voice was in his ear. "We're done. Making an exit." Ben rolled up behind the Subaru allowing the headlights to shine through. Then backed up and pulled away.

"Looks empty," Ben muttered into his com.

As Moshe's vehicle drove out of the garage, Ben pulled behind him and followed to the rendezvous point on the highway. Once again the convoy was heading to Dera Ghazi Khan where they'd separate to take their targets.

"I feel weird." Ben glanced at Elvis. "Even though we're in disguise and all that shit, I feel like someone's been watching us."

"Nah. I thought that Subaru might have been following us, but there was no one in it." Elvis assured him. Even though Elvis said the words, Ben wished he had inspected the car more closely just for peace of mind. He seldom let things like that go, and wondered why he'd let it pass this time. Now he wished he would've tossed it.

"Chances are, it was just my imagination." Ben said aloud, trying to convince himself at this point.

"I don't know, Chief. Wish you would've had me toss it." Elvis read his mind.

Ben thought for a moment. "If we see the same Subaru again, that would be a sure sign and we'll take him out of commission. Or, better, capture the little bastard and find out why he's following us." Ben muttered to Moshe, "If you see that Subaru again, let me know. That just made me feel...funny."

"Could've been the police," Moshe pondered on the com. "They're known to ride undercover at night like that. They probably wondered what we're up to. They'd not stop Humvees, however. Their own military rides around in them constantly. So, they most likely assumed we are military, their own. Hell, our appearance is such. Stop worrying about spooks, Chief. We have bigger fish to fry."

Ben continued driving as the rain abated. Finally. Another few hours and they'd be in Dera Ghazi Khan and the sun would be coming up. The men would split up after spending the day sleeping in a safe house there. Driving through the Afghanistan-Pakistan border area always put everyone on edge. But this time it felt different. Ben couldn't put his finger on it. It was as if someone had a tail on him and now he didn't think it was the Subaru. As the Humvees pulled into the town of Dera Ghazi Khan, he tried to focus on sleeping and eating. The cement factory came into view just before sunrise. Beneath the factory was a protected bunker.

Moshe spoke to the owner, Tarek Noor, a longtime friend, in Urdo. The Humvees rolled inside and the men filed one-by-one into the well-lit chamber beneath the ground. As the city of Dera Ghazi Khan awoke, Moshe's unit and the Dark Horse Guardians slept. Although Ben ate and washed up, he could not relax enough to sleep. Not just yet. He remembered killing a man in this town seven years earlier. The victim had wandered into a skirmish he had no stake in, but Ben mistook him for an enemy. In reality, he would never know if the man was an enemy or an innocent victim of circumstance. But he remembered later the last name was Madi. It was a common name in this region of the world.

Moshe stuck his head into the tiny room, "Get some sleep. You look like hell."

Ben waved him off, "Yeah, right. See you in a few hours." But he knew sleep would not come for a bit longer. The thought of Lara filtered into his mind once or twice as he planned the route he'd take for the coming evening of mayhem. He had to call her. Communicating with her would serve two purposes. One, she'd know he was all right. And, two, he'd know she was, too. But it was deeper than that. He made a silent vow to himself that this would be the last overseas mission. The longing for her was overwhelming at times, so much so, it was pushing him further into the depression he constantly fought. He tapped the satellite phone and listened as it finally rang through. It was early morning where he was, so early evening for Lara. Her cheery voice made him smile.

"Darlin-- I'm just hitting the sack for a few hours, thinking of you, I love you..." he murmured into the satellite phone, wishing he could video chat with her. But that wasn't such a good idea. This would be a short call.

Her response melted him, "Ben, oh Ben...I miss you so much. You're okay? Everything is all right? That's all I need to know. Are you finished?"

"No darlin, but nearly done. I miss kissing you goodnight and eating dinner with you...and Einstein." Oh damn, he felt a lump in his throat. His eyes filled as tears slowly moved down his face. He made the mistake of envisioning Lara there having dinner with Einstein at her feet in the kitchen. For a split second he had allowed himself the luxury of being transported, and knew it was a mistake. He let the tears slide down his face as Lara spoke. "Don't worry about me. I'm fine. Focus on the mission. Monique's with me and Rusty. I just want you safe. I'm thrilled that you called. I can't wait for you to be home, for this to be over. I want you to kiss me and hold me. Tell me everything will be just fine, like you always do." She sounded so normal, so happy to hear from him. He heard her breathing on the other end of the call. The connection had a slight delay, but other than that, it felt as if Lara was in the room with him.

After listening to her sweet, feminine voice filled with excitement, he whispered, "I've got to go. I love you." He heard her say, "I love you, too, Ben." He disconnected. Once more he took her shirt and wiped the tears from his face, hoping none of the men witnessed his emotion. He turned on a map light and studied the GPS coordinates. He remembered the Fort Munro area, even though he'd only passed this way once.

The town of Dera Ghazi Khan served as a junction to the four provinces of Pakistan. Ben's targets lived in the higher elevation setting of Fort Munro away from the dusty, hot climate of Dera Ghazi Khan. Fort

Munro was the only place with clear cool water. It rose over a mile above sea level and brought visitors and residents seeking to escape the heat of the summer. But now it was quiet, isolated. The visiting families and school trips for recreation were not present. This was the winter season. The less people around, the better.

Before sleeping, he moved across the room and Gus was going through the same drill with his map light. "Hey, what's up?"

"You ready for this?" Ben whispered.

"Hell, yeah." Gus smiled. "These bastards are not the usual suspects. They're war criminals, the worst of the worst. I'm more than ready. I mean, Jesus, Ben – its Madi and his band of criminals. I've been waiting for this for a long time. You know what I mean. This is for Sam and Javier and all the bullets all of us have taken along the way. Madi's murderous brother is six-feet under because of you. Yeah. I want these bastards dead."

"I mean are you ready for whatever might happen?" Ben swallowed hard. Gus would be his spotter; they'd worked together a hundred times, maybe more. It was a plain and simple assassination. But nothing was ever plain and simple in this part of the world.

"Yeah. I'm ready. What's the latest intel on our targets?" Gus asked, his blue eyes staring into his.

"They're in the house. We just need to gain entry. They have an elaborate security system but no dogs. You know how these idiots feel about dogs. That's all good for us. I've already looked at what they have for security. I can hack it within a minute. I just want to make sure you are up for the challenge. You know..." Ben rested his hand on the big man's shoulder. "Aw, shit, you are. Goodnight."

Ben watched as Gus curled his long lean body into a ball and fell asleep instantly. He wished the hell he could do that right now. Ben moved to his tiny corner of the room and got comfortable with Lara's shirt wrapped around what was supposed to be a pillow. Ants and cockroaches scurried around the sub-basement in the darkness. Ben couldn't hear them but he could feel them. He left the map light on and it kept some of them at bay.

After ten hours in the underground tomb, the men made their way to the Humvees. The new equipment surpassed their wildest expectations. Wearing the G's at night was like working in the daytime. The clarity and resolution was superior and the com was much improved. The office building of the cement factory had emptied. The workers were gone for the day.

The 275,000 inhabitants of the city were readying themselves for the coming evening. The din of traffic waned and the ritual routines of dinner and bedtime arrived for the masses, as a herd being driven by a dinner bell. Ben sat in stillness, eating, as he watched the sun slip behind the mountainous terrain he'd be navigating in the next few hours. As nighttime fell, the team split up and drove in opposite directions.

There were seven large mosques in the area and the call to prayer was haunting. Every time he heard the mournful chanting, it brought him back to the beginning of it all. His first deployment in Iraq. The years in Afghanistan. Visions flashed through his mind in a second. Dead brothers he could not save. Killing, sleeping, eating, and killing more of them. It seemed he had come full circle. The cities of Iraq and Afghanistan his brothers fought and died for were now overrun with radical Islamists hell bent on a reign of destruction. Screw the Caliphate and the whole damned lot of them. This wasn't religion; it was more like the plague and only men like him were the antidote.

Living amongst the faithful as an undercover adversary for the past few years brought so much to light. The House of Saud was the epicenter for Wahhabism, the strict doctrine of Islamic faith. He sucked in a deep breath and let it out slowly, remembering the horrors brought upon the world because of this purveyor of evil. He clearly understood why eliminating them was so easy. It was kill or be killed in their sick twisted world. He had witnessed the slaughter of thousands of innocent Christians, Jews, Kurds, or other Muslims who chose not to follow their horrific doctrine, if it could even be called that, for the very word doctrine implied principles. There were no principles involved, as he recalled the vivid images of dead bodies tortured and mutilated. Those images were always in his mind just before he pulled the trigger or plunged the knife. Yes, they made it easy to kill them.

"You okay, Chief?" Gus spoke, bringing him out of a bloody reverie.

"Yeah, good. Let's do this." Ben glanced at the satellite image on his phone and read the latest text message. "They're right where we want them right now. Let's hope they stay put."

Gus managed a tight-lipped smile, "Let's hope." He grabbed his HK M23 and plenty of ammo, and a Sig Sauer P226 for back-up.

The battered vehicle they drove was not built for speed or agility, but it blended in with the landscape and the populace. The Chevy pick-up from the cement factory was not bulletproof. In fact, it was rusty and more than ten years old, but had two new tires in the bed covering their gear. Ben held the MK11 sniper rifle with a 20 round mag, QD scope rings, and a high definition mil-dot laser. He'd affix the swivel-base bipod on a mount and attach the sound suppressor once they found the right spot to set up. The free-floating 20 inch barrel and rail accessory system allowed for extreme accuracy. Although this weapon fired a 7.62 round, it was not capable of fully automatic fire. But this was his go-to sniper rifle for many years. It was so comfortable, it felt like part of his body while a Navy SEAL deployed in the Middle East. His best shot had been in Ramadi at a forward operating base. He hit a target in the chest as far away as 1,500 yards.

Approaching the fig orchard, Gus parked the truck and the two silently unloaded and strapped on every piece of gear in total darkness. The ground was saturated and muddy from the heavy rain. Their G's were attached and checked. The two made their way closer to the house which was barely visible through the thicket of trees and outbuildings. Every so often, they'd stop and listen for any sound other than that of nature. There was a stillness in the mountains, and the only noise was that of their footsteps making soft sucking sounds in the mud. Ben checked his phone for the weather again. The rain had passed and he was relieved it was a windless night. This always enhanced target accuracy.

Waving his right arm, Gus found the spot. Moving slowly, methodically, Gus built a blind to cover himself and Ben moved around to the East side of the house. Several vehicles were parked there and Ben immediately recognized one – the Subaru. There were many Subaru cars and SUV's driven in this part of the world, but this one stood out for some reason. Maybe because it was red, the same color as the one he had seen earlier. Or maybe in the darkness he was imagining it was the same color.

Turning toward the hillside that was at the foot of a mountain, he made the ascent to a flat spot with good cover and set up shop. He laid out the 20-round magazines and fixed the tripod taking time to breathe and relax while attending to the finest details.

"Hey." He heard Gus breathe over the com.

"What." Ben answered.

"It's that Subaru."

"Not sure it's the same one," Ben replied.

"Yeah, it is."

"Maybe we'll find out who the hell's driving it." Ben answered.

Movement, side door," Gus whispered. "It's show time."

According to the intel, there were five terrorists meeting in the house, but there were six vehicles parked out front. Ben had the M11 ready to rip. He waited patiently as Gus employed the decoy. Not wanting to draw fire from the targets, Gus played a recording of a female's voice pleading for help in Urdu dialect. He had tossed a synthetic human-like form onto the front yard area wearing what appeared to be a white dress. It was hoped the men would think the commotion was a young woman in some sort of distress.

"Hold on, Chief." Gus uttered. "They're sending out a kid."

To Ben's dismay, a young child of six or seven stepped into the front yard and made his way to the fake female form lying on the ground before him. A voice yelled to the child from the building, "What is it, Yusef?" The child yelled back, but Ben couldn't understand his answer. Gus allowed the woman's voice to project into the darkness. Everyone seemed to be collectively holding their breath as two men exited the side door of the house facing Ben.

The young boy was now standing at the form of the woman, touching her garment. Through the night vision scope, Ben could see the child's eyelashes. He was gauging his reaction. The boy seemed to think he was seeing a ghost, and jumped back from the form on the ground after fingering the gauzy fabric. The two men were now ten yards from the boy and three other figures were emerging from the doorway.

"Now," Gus commanded.

"Got it." Ben squeezed the trigger hitting the two of the men emerging from the doorway. By the time the third man realized what was happening, he had turned to go back inside. Ben swung, took his aim, and shot him center mass. Meanwhile, one man, ran around the house, dashed toward a different doorway and got inside. Within seconds, the child scrambled through the doorway and it closed. Gus had taken down one man, very near to the child.

"Shit," Ben hissed.

"The kid ran into the house." Gus stated the obvious. "And the last guy is in there, too."

"Got to go." Ben was already closing up shop at his sniper position and moving for his pistol.

What happened next was not expected. There was no movement in the house for at least ten minutes as Gus and Ben moved slowly back to the hidden pick-up truck. Without warning, the young boy emerged without sound from the fig grove pointing a Kalashnikov AK47 at Ben. The man standing behind him trained an HK P9S on Gus.

"Jesus." Ben whispered. But before anyone fired a shot, Ben and Gus dove toward their adversaries in the black of night. The AK47 fired and dropped to the ground as Ben secured the young boy. The HK pistol went off grazing Gus, drawing blood, but he took the man off his feet.

Gus glanced nervously at Ben, "Now what…"

"We'll bind them up and get the hell out of here. They don't know who we are." Ben uttered frantically. As they rapidly wound rope around the hands and feet of the two, they simultaneously muffled any noise with a bandana stuffed into their mouths, secured with a bungee cord.

"That'll hold them for a few minutes. We've got to get some photos and run. The cavalry will be here soon. I'm sure they've made a phone call. Grab their phones." Ben's heart was racing. Gus did so, as Ben photographed the faces of the four dead men. As he gazed one last time at the young man on the ground with the kid, he did not recognize him as a target.

"Who the hell are you?" Ben uttered, mystified for a second. Gus was in the truck and it was rolling. Ben ran alongside and hopped in. "I hope I just didn't just make a big mistake."

"I didn't want to kill the kid," Gus said. "The other guy, maybe. Let's take him with us." Gus pulled a U-turn and Ben dragged the bound man into the truck bed. He hopped back in. "We need to fly. We can't hang around. No time now. Gus floor it!"

The old truck took off in the darkness spewing mud everywhere behind it. Ben kept an eye on the unknown person bound and gagged in the back, covered with gear getting bumped around, but he was secured to the truck bed. They took a westerly route which was different than the path they took to get there. Now the targets were killed, and they had an unknown to interrogate. Their piece of the mission was completed.

Ben breathed a sigh of relief. "Let's take this guy to the cement factory."

"No," Gus was somber. "There's a cave about two clicks from here. I remember it well. We can take him there."

"Don't like it. Too uncertain." I'm asking Moshe. Tapping his com, Moshe's voice came over the speaker. "Yeah."

"What is the plan for interrogation?" Ben asked.

"Go to the pit stop. You remember that place?" Moshe replied.

"Yes, that crappy little dirt road that ends in the valley...I've got it. Is that still there? Didn't expect to pick this guy up, but he might be of some value," Ben informed him.

"Didn't expect you to capture anyone, but that's the place for doing what you need to do. I'll call ahead, there are two guys from my unit on stand-by there. I'll let them know you're coming." Moshe stated.

Gus laughed, "This shit doesn't get easier. In fact, it gets crazier every time. Why didn't we know about the kid and the other guy? Our intel sucked on this one, Chief."

"We'll discuss that in the debrief, you can be certain." Ben ran his hand over his face and looked at his hand. Everything, including the truck was covered with mud, and his face was, too. The black truck and mud-covered men pulled onto the long and winding dirt road leading to the pit-stop. The only thing Ben didn't like about this location was there was only one road going in. He preferred to have options if a quick exit was needed.

The ramshackle building from ten years ago was still standing. Ben and Elvis pulled the prisoner out of the truck bed along with some gear and knocked on the steel door. Within seconds it opened and they entered what was a steel building that had seen better days. It was now covered with overgrown vines and mud from the recent rain.

"What do we have here?" one of Moshe's men asked, as his eyes roamed over the prisoner.

"We don't know. We didn't expect him to be at the party. There was a kid, too. He pointed a gun at us, but we bound and gagged the kid and left him there. This one we decided to take. He may have some information." Ben searched through the photographs of terrorists on his phone again...and compared each one to the man's face lying on the floor. "Nope. None of these matches. So, now we need to find out who the hell he is and what information we can extract from him, if any."

Chapter 9

~Abdul Rahman Shafir~

Although he knew he'd be kicked and beaten by the infidels, Abdul remained motionless on the floor of the building. He had chosen a false name to give these fools, and would feign ignorance even if they beat him to a bloody pulp. He had been beaten before by Salib Madi, his father, his superior, the man he wanted more than ever to impress. He was told the whippings would make him stronger, more resilient when it came time to fight these men he so wanted to kill.

The tall man with deep blue eyes removed the gag from his mouth. The man glanced at his phone repeatedly as his eyes took in the details of his face. Abdul felt uncomfortable being scrutinized in this fashion and averted his eyes. He knew now that this was Keegan, the man they'd been hunting for years. He'd sensed it in the Subaru when he pulled behind them in Bhakkar. He also knew the man had a family in America, a woman, with dark hair who was beautiful. And she was being followed and might even be captured by now. It was difficult to keep the smile from coming to his lips, but he remained still and kept his eyes closed. He knew more than the blue-eyed man, but he had to remain quiet.

A chair was pushed to the wall and the blue-eyed man picked him up with one arm and set him in the chair like a rag doll. Then he leaned in closer, and began asking him questions in Urdu. He understood every word the man was saying, but shrugged his shoulders, pretending he did not understand. The longer he could play this game, the more likely it would be he'd be allowed to leave. They'd figure he was a goat herder visiting the house of the men they killed. Maybe. Or, they could beat him bloody senseless trying to get information out of him. Either way, he wasn't talking. He remained in the chair for several hours, as he watched the four men in the room. He understood English perfectly and absorbed every word they said.

The blue-eyed man returned and gave him a drink out of a bottle of water. Then sat next to him in a chair, as if he wanted to be friendly.

Abdul couldn't believe he was sitting next to the man who had killed so many of his tribe, the devil himself. The American soldier they had talked about since he could remember. The man gave him a few bites to eat. Then he smiled. Abdul would always remember the details of his face. His blue eyes and thick dark hair would stay in his memory. He spoke with a strange accent.

"What is your name?" the blue-eyed man asked. Abdul gave no response, just shrugged.

The man spoke in several different dialects, including Punjabi, Arabic, and Urdu, but Abdul pretended he did not comprehend.

"Come on, my friend. We don't want this to get ugly now, do we?" the man spoke closely to his ear. He could smell his breath and he had just eaten onions. His blue eyes looked tired as he turned to his partner, "Gus, you want to talk with him?"

The other man, very tall and blonde, came and sat in the chair facing him now. He had blue eyes, too, but they were cold and calculating as they searched Abdul's face making a shiver run down his spine. The tall man reached out and slapped him across the face hard. Abdul pretended he was fearful, even managed to start crying. Another slap, then another. But anything they did would not make him talk. He sobbed like a baby for a while, hoping to gain some sympathy.

A few hours later, another man interrogated him. Then another. It went on for several hours and Abdul took several beatings but did not speak.

At one point, the man named Gus said he thought that he was possibly deaf and mute. "He might be a goat herder. We don't have him on our radar. I say we kick him. We've got to get the hell out of here as soon as it's dark."

Abdul was released in the middle of the night. The men named Gus and Tom took him for a ride. Abdul's hands were bound, but he was released and he ran like the wind. He couldn't wait to tell his father he knew where Ben Keegan was.

~ Saleh Ali ~

It seemed since birth Saleh was always cleaning up after his half-brother, Abdul. Until Saleh arrived in a white sedan with his father, Salib Madi, he had no idea what had taken place at the house where his father's henchmen were having their meeting. He rode in his father's white Mercedes this time because he was training to be a lieutenant in the Islamic state's army. Pulling up on the scene, he had no idea what had happened. He only heard the other men talking about a shoot-out. Seven other Islamic soldiers were close behind, six of them with AR's strapped to their bodies. The men and ammo filled the back of an ancient Ford pick-up.

As Madi exited the white Mercedes, he ordered Yusef, the young boy, untied. He spat questions at the child. "Who were these men? Tell me everything. Did you take a photo of them with your phone? Did they leave anything behind?"

Yusef dutifully explained what happened, right up to the part where he and Abdul held the men captive with guns for a moment. Saleh watched as Madi's eyes filled with fury and they seemed to bore through the child. "What? You had the chance to shoot these men and you let them go? Which gun did you have, Yusef. Tell me."

Yusef couldn't stop the uncontrollable convulsions that overtook his body and he fell to his knees and vomited at Salib Madi's feet. Madi's heavy foot pushed the young boy over in one swift motion. "You coward. What is wrong with you?"

Yusef rallied and stood up. He reached for the long gun. "This one." Yusef exclaimed, holding up the AK47, his dark eyes seeking approval. Salib Madi took the AK away from Yusef and shot him in the head. The small boy stumbled backward as blood drained from his shattered skull and he fell to the ground twitching once or twice.

"Do you see? This is how you kill someone." Madi scooped up the pistol that he found lying on the ground and put it in his belt while he spoke to the dead child lying on the ground before him. "You little fool. I gave you the chance to be a man, a fighter. I cannot have incompetent idiots working for me." Madi turned to his men, "Now you will have to find Abdul. This Keegan is making things much more difficult."

Saleh stood shivering as Madi grabbed his arm and shoved him toward the boy's dead body. "Stop shaking. Clean this up, like a man, if you want to be an Islamic jihadist. You are weak like a woman. Afraid of everything!" Saleh watched as a gob of spit landed on the face of the boy as Madi moved past the lifeless body. He could no longer stand there risking his own safety. He knew he had to find the courage and stamina to do as he was told.

"Let Saleh Ali clean up the mess." Madi got into the white sedan and sped off but continued giving orders to Saleh on his phone.

Saleh could hear Madi's orders on the speaker. "Get the security feed. The cameras must have captured some images we can use." Madi was ranting wildly now and the men were jumping at his every command. Upon closer examination one of the soldiers murmured in Urdu dialect, "The cameras did not record....anything.....they stopped working after 9 PM..."

Madi screamed into the phone at Saleh, "Is that the time they were here? The devils must have done something to the cameras. "Randee ka bacha," Saleh listened as Madi lost control. Calling him a son of a whore didn't matter. Madi was his father even though he had killed his mother long ago. He was bound to this man forever and would serve him. He silently chastised himself for even being born. His life was one of service to a madman.

Since the day he was born, Saleh did as he was told, and this moment would be no different. A jihadist with a black scarf wound around his face picked up the body of the boy and tossed him like a sack of rice into the back of the pick-up. Saleh covered Yusef's dead body with a blanket, attempting a modicum of dignity. It should not have surprised him to watch his father put a bullet through his younger brother's head. It wasn't the first relative he'd witnessed being shot. But for a moment he questioned everything his father did. He joined the men in the bed of the pick-up truck. Sitting above the wheel well, Saleh's eyes traveled over these men his father admired so much. Killers. Executioners. These were *real* men, his father would say. And, somehow Saleh had to find a way to measure up. The only way would be to find the man his father wanted dead: Lieutenant Ben Keegan.

Abdul and Yusef had Keegan right there with a gun aimed at him, yet they hesitated a split second before pulling the trigger. Why? He chastised himself over and over for allowing Yusef to be used in this manner. He was too young. The truck sped toward the compound. If he didn't dispose of Yusef's body immediately, he knew he would be in for further punishment. What just happened was only the public humiliation. There would be much worse to come later when they were alone.

The truck stopped and the men jumped off, scrambling to a tent to eat and be cared for by the women. For a moment, Saleh stayed in the back with Yusef's lifeless body. Flies now buzzing around, he slid into the driver's seat after grabbing a shovel and continued driving to the dirt road in the valley. It was a remote place but appropriate for a quiet burial. At least no one would disturb Yusef in death, he thought. In some ways, Saleh thought Yusef was the lucky one. He was gone now to wherever the human spirit goes after death. His short life had been violent and void of love. Saleh wondered what love even was. He had heard about it, but the only love he had experienced was brief with his mother as a very young child and with his half-brother, Yusef, when they played. He could barely remember those times, now. Tears slid down his face as he dug his younger brother's grave.

As he lowered Yusef's wrapped body into the grave he had dug, he felt a hand around his throat from behind. Two men had appeared out of nowhere with blackened faces. A bag was slipped over his head. He was bound and dragged a long distance. He felt a doorway open and heard it close. The Americans were speaking to one another. When the blue-eyed man took the bag off and looked at Saleh's face he quickly pulled his phone up and scrolled through photos.

"Bingo!' he heard the man say as he smiled. Saleh had never heard that word before, even though he'd been schooled in English. The blue-eyed man was smiling.

~ Ben ~

"If my eyes are not deceiving me, we've got one of Salib Madi's men here." Ben smiled at Bettencourt, Elvis, Tom and Gus. "He should be a goldmine of information." Ben detected the wild-eyed panic in Saleh's eyes and searched him thoroughly while his hands were bound. Then he and Elvis quickly tied him to a chair and began asking questions.

"What were you doing out there just now?" Ben began. He noticed the young man's black eyes were shuttered against him, averted, and he was trembling slightly.

Elvis spoke for him, "He was burying a kid."

"Did you kill that young boy?" Ben asked. He detected strong defiance in this young man's eyes when they met his. The question struck a chord. Ben guessed his age to be twenty, maybe slightly younger.

"No, I didn't kill him." Saleh answered, then his eyes moved to the floor.

"Who's the kid?" Ben continued, sensing this was a delicate subject. But there was no answer from Saleh.

"Your name, it's Saleh Ali, we know who you are." Ben informed him.

"I'm not talking to you or anyone else," Saleh reacted, eyes still glued to the floor.

"We can make you talk," Ben countered, hoping for the defiant look to return and it did.

Saleh's eyes met his, "You can't make me do anything."

Ben rummaged around in a rucksack and found a straightjacket. "I think this will fit you perfectly." After allowing Saleh a moment to drink some water and urinate, the jacket was forced upon him and snugged up. "We've got to get the hell out of here. He's going with us, but we need to cover him well. A rag was stuffed into Saleh's mouth and he was stowed in the back of the vehicle's front seat, on the floor, then covered with another blanket.

Ben laughed. "He looks like a mummy."

The men exited the building and drove by the site of the burial that was not completed. Elvis stopped for five minutes and shoveled the rest of the dirt onto the grave and hopped back into the truck as it remained idling. "He's buried."

Before daylight they made their way back to Dera Ghazi Khan and the bunker beneath the cement factory. Saleh was blindfolded and remained very quiet, Ben observed. He wondered just how much this young man knew and began to develop a plan to interrogate him. The young boy he was burying had some meaning to him, and he must have felt the truck stop and heard the shoveling sounds as they finished the grave properly. This would be the starting point. Ben would handle this young man differently than all the rest. He knew there was a strong connection to Salib Madi, the major terrorist kingpin they were hunting. But how could he get to him?

The men were getting settled while the day above ground began. There was little sound in the bunker, except that of the trucks rumbling above and the continual grinding and growling of the cement making equipment. Ben scrolled through the pictures on his phone one more time, looking at Madi then at Saleh. There was a slight resemblance. It was the eyes.

~ Lara ~

Panic set in as she searched outside for the detectives charged with watching over her. She sent them a text but no answer. Her first instinct was to contact Rusty.

His familiar voice answered on the first ring, "What's up?"

Lara whispered into the phone, "The detectives are nowhere to be seen. I have an awful feeling, you know, hackles."

"Not a good sign. Call the department?" Rusty asked.

"No. I haven't yet. Maybe it's just my imagination. The detectives might be purposefully out of sight. But I sent a text to them and got no answer. That made me think something might have happened."

"I'll be there in a few minutes. Leaving right now." Rusty uttered and his phone went dead.

Lara ruminated for a moment. If, in fact, something happened to the detectives, she had to call the head of the detective division. She dialed the number and heard his curt voice. "Redman."

"It's Mrs. Keegan."

Redman answered, "Yes, ma'am. How can I help you?"

"The detectives are nowhere to be seen. I tried to contact them, but no answer."

A loud noise outside interrupted her call. Monique's eyes met Lara's for a second.

"They're here...get someone to help me," Lara whispered into the phone and ended the call. She grabbed her handgun off her hip.

She motioned to Monique to move into the middle guest room upstairs and told her to close the door. "Get on the floor, behind the dresser and stay there, no matter what you hear." Lara slid open a drawer and pulled out another gun, handing it to Monique muzzle down.

"Take this. It's a Smith and Wesson revolver, it's loaded. Don't point it at anyone unless you're going to pull the trigger. If they make it past me, you kill them. So, go upstairs and keep the barrel pointed away from you. Got it? I'm coming right up behind you and will set up in the window."

Lara knew her best shot would be from upstairs, and drew her Glock19 and waited, pressing her body against the wall for cover. She listened as the men set off the security alarm. The steel door made it difficult to gain entry so they broke a window and entered that way. They had to know it would only be minutes before police would arrive.

Lara could hear them as they walked from the kitchen through the dining room and into the living room. The television was still on low, but she could hear their voices. As she caught a glimpse of them moving beneath the staircase. She saw the face of Aaron Brown. They had weapons visible. They were here to kill her. They'd killed Officer Simpson. She took a deep breath and let it out. There would be no warning, as Rusty had taught her, just aim and pull the trigger.

As the two men stepped onto the first stair, she peeked around the corner. They had guns drawn. She would have to be fast to hit them both center mass, or it would be mayhem.

Lara slid down the wall to shrink her target profile, then wheeled around in a crouch, gun raised.

The nice thing about stairs is that they created a perfect bottleneck. The area of maneuverability would be limited. These jerks had nowhere to run, nowhere to hide. Shooting down the stairs, blindly, she'd be almost certain to hit some part of someone. Shooting straight down the middle would almost guarantee a hit.

But, she wasn't blind firing. At this distance, she could put two nice neat holes in Tim's head. Instead, she went for the more reliable shot in the center of his chest. She pulled the trigger.

Tim's body met the impact of the bullets and staggered. He took a step back down the stairs, and Aaron caught him before Tim could fall any further.

At that moment, with Tim bleeding profusely atop Aaron, Lara observed two things very clearly.

One, Tim held an MP5k-PDW submachinegun, a dangerous weapon for her to contend with.

Two, there was no blood on Tim's chest — he was wearing Kevlar.

Lara dove back behind the cover of the wall as Tim opened up with a stream of fully-automatic fire. Thankfully, automatic fire was difficult to aim even if you *didn't* feel as though you'd been punched in the chest by sheet metal.

She heard the three-round burst fired on semi-automatic. That must have been Aaron. She silently chastised herself for not taking the headshot when she had the opportunity.

Then something surprising happened; they retreated.

Lara wasn't going to have that. She charged down the stairs, gun low and by her side, and took up a Weaver stance by the doorway. She shot at them as they hopped into a different vehicle, which looked like a Dodge Charger, and squealed tires out of the driveway. She fired single, carefully placed rounds until her magazine ran dry.

"Damn it!" she yelled.

Ten minutes elapsed before several police cars, Rusty and his friend, Carter, converged on the scene. "Good job, Mrs. Keegan." The responding officers touched her shoulder. "Are you all right, ma'am?"

"Yes. I'm fine. What happened to the detectives guarding us?" Lara asked. She could tell by Rusty's demeanor the answer wasn't going to be a good one.

"We found them in the side yard. Dead, ma'am. We'll do ballistics and set up the crime scene for analysis, but it's pretty obvious what happened here. They killed the two detectives outside. We believe they're the same suspects in Officer Simpson's death. You're a brave woman."

"Just pissed."

"Copy that."

The crime scene experts arrived, and Lara sat on a chair in the kitchen feeling numb.

Rusty brought a weeping Monique out of the upstairs guest room. Monique was shivering and repeated, "Lara, what happened to Lara?"

"She is okay, it's over." Lara heard Rusty speaking calmly as he put his arm around Monique's shoulder. "It's all right now." Lara listened to his soothing voice, wishing she could be lulled into a sense of security right now, but knew better.

In the kitchen at Clearwater Farm, they walked through the details.

She sensed that Rusty was on high alert as he spoke calmly, methodically, calculating the next move. "If these two guys know where Ben lives, most likely there are others who have this information. Pack a bag and drive up to Wisdom Lake for the next few days. It's cold outside and the Lake is frozen, but Alvin's got it nice and toasty up there."

The plan was for Rusty's friend, Carter, to wear a long dark wig, which Rusty had cleverly brought with him, and he'd drive Lara's Mercedes in a southerly direction on Interstate 95. Lara, Monique, and Rusty would take Carter's Jeep Cherokee on a long four-hour drive north to a place few people knew existed. To get a head start, Carter, slipped on the long, dark wig, and Lara's coat. Mimicking her body movements, he hopped into Lara's Mercedes and started driving south. Within forty minutes, Rusty had a text from him. "Being followed. Will give them a long run."

Lara's phone rang, and she listened to Captain Redman as he gave her details. "Mrs. Keegan, it might be best if you could lay low for a while. Do you have another place you could stay for a few days until we gather more information? From what we can tell, the leak was from someone in the State Department to a terror cell – the Islamic State – ma'am – are you there?"

Lara exhaled, "Oh God, the State Department? What about Ben? Will he be safe? How much detail was leaked?"

Redman paused, then said, "Ben's name and home address was included in the data. This makes you a target. Can you get far away to a secluded location?"

Lara didn't like his tone, it raised her hackles. "Yes, I can. In fact, I'm heading out now." Einstein licked her face as he leaned against her. "I have guns and plenty of ammo. I will keep out of sight until I hear from you Captain Redman."

"Good." Redman seemed relieved. "I'll be in touch. We know your husband, ma'am and respect him greatly. Please know, we will do everything within our power to get as much information as we can to contain the situation. Talk soon."

The call ended and even though Lara felt she should have faith in Captain Redman, she didn't. She couldn't even trust the federal government, and she was supposed to trust the local government? Good Lord. The State Department. She couldn't imagine how or why this happened and wanted answers.

Rusty looked at her, "Are you thinking what I'm thinking?"

Lara exhaled, "You want to come, too."

"Yup." He muttered solemnly. "I've got a stash of clothing and supplies up there. Let's go."

After packing a few belongings, Monique and Lara got into the Jeep Cherokee as Rusty pulled onto Interstate 95 heading north to a destination located somewhere between Mud Pond and Wisdom Lake....off the map, so to speak. Off the grid. Rusty drove as Lara sent a text to the caretaker, Alvin. *See you in four hours or so. Urgently need to see you for a taxidermy project.*

The text back simply said, *Yup.*

Chapter 10

Pakistan

~ Ben ~

It was the last chance to extract information from Saleh. Ben would pull out the stops. There was something about this young man, he couldn't decipher it just yet – but the young boy he was in the process of burying meant something to him. Ben had to get the details -- get inside his head.

After sleeping and eating, Ben allowed his prisoner to use the bathroom with him standing at the doorway. His plan seemed to be working. By not interrogating Saleh immediately and roughing him up, the young man seemed to be softening, just a little. He'd made eye contact with him a couple of times while eating.

It was a wretched place, really, the bunker beneath the cement factory. No frills, but a tiny private room gave him the solitude he needed. Ben glanced at his phone with the knowledge he had exactly two hours before the team had to be packed and out of there. The other men were loading up, getting ready to leave as darkness descended above ground.

He found the photos of William on his phone, and kept Saleh bound to a chair in the small room. This question and answer session would be different. He showed the photo of William to Saleh. "This is my son." Ben scrolled through six or seven photos of William slowly.

He watched as Saleh's eyes roamed over the photos and could tell he was gauging the age of the child. "How old was the boy you were burying?" Ben asked gently. He watched Saleh's demeanor soften, and imagined he was recalling the task of shoveling dirt onto the boy's body when the Dark Horse Guardians snatched him.

"How old is the boy in the photo, your son?" Saleh asked predictably.

"He just turned ten." Ben said. "I miss him very much. As a soldier, I do not get to see my son very often, but I love him. He means a lot to me. Soon, he will be a man. I have many things to teach him. A father is important in a young man's life."

Saleh's eyes changed at the mention of a father...there was a hardening, a defiance. Saleh averted his eyes. Ben sensed there was something there. Not sure what, he continued to probe. Ben continued, "I love my father. I want my son to love me the same way. And, to respect me."

"Respect." Saleh nearly spat the word. "I do not understand that term."

"What is your father like?" Ben asked quietly.

"My father is not someone I want to talk about." Saleh turned away.

"What has he done to make you feel this way?" Ben continued.

Saleh was silent but thinking. Ben sensed this young man had tumultuous emotions running through him.

"How old are you, Saleh?" Ben asked.

"Seventeen." Saleh answered flatly. "I am no longer a boy and haven't been for a long time."

"When did you become a man?" Ben queried.

"When I killed my first infidel." Saleh answered. "You must understand. I do not love my father, and I do not respect my father. I obey him."

"Is that what happened to the young boy. You killed him and buried him because you were obeying your father?" Ben was now fishing for answers.

"No." Saleh's eyes were defiant as they met Ben's. "My father killed him. He was my brother. I took care of him when my mother died. It was my responsibility to bury him, properly. Just like I buried my mother. She was twenty when she died. Only three years older than I am right now."

For a moment, Ben was taken aback by the brutality of the scene Saleh most likely witnessed. "You saw this happen?"

Saleh's eyes welled with the beginning of tears, but he suddenly turned away. "I don't want to talk about this."

"I have a feeling you hate your father, but you don't dare to say the words." Ben was right there at the edge, he could feel it. Saleh was going to tell him everything.

Ben opened a bottle of Coke and gave Saleh a drink. He said it was his favorite drink. After a few gulps, his dark eyes met Ben's. "My father is a killer. I am afraid he will kill me, especially after this. That's if you don't kill me first."

"I don't want to kill you, Saleh." Ben stated. "In fact, I think you are an intelligent young man."

"Not really..." Saleh replied. "Abdul is the intelligent one."

"Who is Abdul?" Ben asked.

"And, Ibrahim. He is favored, too," Saleh replied, his eyes glassy as if remembering something.

"Who is Ibrahim?" Ben quizzed.

Then, as if a flurry of emotion hit him, Saleh began talking. Ben listened as the young man before him erupted with a passionate diatribe. "Abdul and Ibrahim are my older brothers. But, we have different mothers. My mother is dead. Their mother is alive. They are charged with finding you, Keegan. There's a bounty on your head, half million. Abdul and Ibrahim told my father they have found you, or someone close to you. That is why he favors them. My father said they are real men, and I am not." Saleh hung his head as if he was ashamed to continue.

"Where is Abdul, where is Ibrahim?" Ben continued prodding. "Come on, Saleh. Tell me."

"They're following you. I don't know where they are right now," Saleh said, defeated.

"Listen to me," Ben started. "I have a deal for you, if you want to do it. Are you interested?"

"What deal?" Saleh's head lifted slightly.

"I will turn you loose and not speak of capturing you, but I need something in return."

Saleh's demeanor brightened as a man who had just escaped the hangman's noose. "What do you need?"

"Information. You contact me. Let me know what Abdul, Ibrahim, and your father are doing every day. I will give you a phone number. But you would need to be able to deceive – do you understand? You would need to be smart, resourceful, creative….do you think you could do that?"

Ben could see Saleh's mind churning. His life was on the line. There was something else he wanted, but Ben didn't know what it was. Then he said it. "My father. I want him dead. Do you understand? No one can know this."

"Trust me, this can be done, and no one will know you had anything to do with it. I need information. I will be your only contact. Before you leave, I need to know everything about Abdul and Ibrahim and your father. Every detail you can give me." Ben exhaled. The deal was made and the information dump began in earnest.

Forty minutes later he pulled Moshe aside. "He's going to be an informant. I'm cutting him loose."

Ben saw shocked horror in Moshe's eyes. "Have you lost your mind? This kid has seen us. He could identify us. He knows too much. We either kill him or take him prisoner. I don't want to let him go."

"I seldom argue with you, but I know this is the right thing to do. This kid detests his father. The young boy he was burying was his brother. He watched his old man pump bullets into his little brother's brain. If that's not motivation, I don't know what is. Plus, he's given me a boatload of information about his father, Salib Madi and his two older brothers. Jesus, this will make your blood run cold." Ben shoved the notes in front of Moshe. "Read some of this."

After a few minutes of reading, Moshe locked eyes with Ben's. "We've got to get the hell out of here in a few minutes. If you really think this is going to work, then go ahead and kick him. But does he understand what will happen to him if he doesn't live up to his end of the bargain?"

"Yeah. I told him he'd be dead. And, he'd never know where or how or who, but it would happen." Ben stated matter-of-factly.

"All right. Let's get out of this shithole as soon as possible. You take Saleh on a little ride, but bring some of the guys with you and don't venture too far."

"I'll be back in fifteen." Ben said. He collected Saleh, still bound. Then quickly strapped on body armor and a few weapons. A pick-up truck from the cement facility was borrowed. Ben, Elvis, Tom and Saleh rode about ten miles down the paved road and pulled over. There was very little light, except for the slight glimmer of the stars and moon. In the headlights, Ben cut Saleh loose and hopped back in the truck.

As he turned the truck around, he glanced at the reflection of Saleh in the rearview mirror. The defiant young man walked on, without looking back. Riding back to the cement plant, Ben hoped to God he was doing the right thing. The men were eerily silent. They parked the truck, got out and tossed their gear into the Humvees. It was time to head toward the border in the black of night, never a good feeling.

While driving toward the Pakistani border, Ben's phone vibrated S.O.S. and he knew immediately it was Rusty. "Yeah." The vehicle was bouncing all over the place and the men in the background were noisy. Ben cupped the phone and shouted, "Quiet!" He didn't like the fact that Rusty was calling him. It never was good news when he got a phone call from him while on a mission.

"Listen." Rusty said. "Lara and Monique are being tracked by American jihadists here. They're at the black site until further notice. Heads up -- the leak came from the State Department."

Ben muttered profanities, but knew being frustrated right now wouldn't serve him well. "Protect them. I'll be back soon. I just got some bad news about Nazmin. She was one of my best contacts in Pakistan; she was murdered. It was brutal. The bastards put it on YouTube. Can't let this go."

"Damn." He heard Rusty mutter. "Don't worry about us. I can get the girls to a safe place. You know where I'm going."

"Thanks, take care you're not being tailed." Ben reminded him, but knew he didn't have to.

"Got it covered, Chief." Rusty said plainly. "Catch you later."

At the end of the call, Ben felt as if things were falling apart. It was the intel leak. All of Lara's hard work to stop it was for naught.

~ Lara ~

Four hours later with no stopping, Rusty finally turned down the winding unused road leading to the black site. Lara was thankful that they were in a four-wheel drive Jeep Cherokee, as the road had been plowed by a front-end loader, but lots of snow remained, creating frozen ruts. The ride was bumpy and slow; once or twice an animal's eyes shone into the headlights. Lara glanced at Monique, whose attention was fixed on the windshield.

"Where the hell are we?" Monique asked plaintively, sounding exhausted.

"We're here." Lara smiled. "Don't worry."

"Who's worried? I could never find this place. I still can't even see it." Monique replied as they got out of the vehicle.

Rusty parked the Jeep behind the thicket and covered it with loose pine branches, as Lara, Monique and Einstein walked around outside. The hoot of an owl nearly made Monique jump out of her skin. Einstein was sniffing the ground around the steel hut, a smorgasbord of smells, Lara imagined. After stretching their legs, Alvin Nichols, the caretaker, greeted them.

"Got some stew cookin' in there for ya, on the woodstove....got bread, too." Alvin gave them a toothy grin. He was at least seventy, but the old Viet Nam vet was lanky and strong with a full head of snow white hair. He held the door for them to enter, then bolted it securely behind them.

Alvin seemed happy to have visitors. He ladled stew into wooden bowls and carved up a large loaf of bread. "Made that bread myself. Love homemade bread." He set the table and poured spring water from a pitcher.

Lara made herself comfortable at the worn wooden table and was amazed at the level of cleanliness in the kitchen. Alvin insisted they sit and eat while he waited on them. The stew was delicious and Rusty had a second helping.

"What is this? It's delicious," Monique whispered to Lara.

"Moose meat stew," Alvin answered with a smile. "It's good and lean, much better for ya than beef." Lara caught Monique's eyes and held them, as if telling her to be quiet.

"This bread is delicious," Lara said, meaning every word. The whole meal was tasty.

After eating, Alvin took them down to the end of the hut where there were six bunks freshly made. "Here's where ya sleep. And, the toilet is a composting one. Makes a bit of noise, but its right here through the door. Only way to wash up is in an old copper bathtub. I'll fill it in the morning for ya. I've got a kettle of hot water on the woodstove. Well, I'll let ya all get some sleep. It's late and I'm sure you're tired."

With that, he moved down to the kitchen area, where his bunk was, and shut off the gas light. The battery-powered lantern was the only light in the bunk area and it was now turned off to conserve energy. Lara was so tired, she kicked off her boots, removed her coat and crawled into the bunk. She tried her best to ignore the taxidermied heads of animals adorning the walls, staring down at her. Monique and Rusty did the same. Within ten minutes Rusty was snoring and Monique was sound asleep. Moonlight glowed around the edges of the window covered by a thermal shade. Lara took a deep breath, exhaled, and closed her eyes. Einstein was cuddled up against her back and she could feel his bull-dog breath on her. For a moment, a feeling of safety flooded over her. She imagined what Ben was doing. She could not fight the sleep that overpowered her. She hadn't felt such exhaustion for a long time.

~ Ben ~

The city of Khost, just over the border in Afghanistan, would be their last stop. Information gathered from Saleh gave Ben the hope for one more brief mission. *Find this Abdul bastard that brutally and publicly murdered Nazmin.* The men were hardened when they found out their friend and informant died in such a gruesome manner. Nazmin was loved by them, and they revered her for risking her life to save many others. She had been a fount of intel, but Salib Madi somehow discovered she was helping them. The intel leak revealed her name, thus making her a target for Madi and his band of marauders. But Moshe was having none of it right now. Taking out Abdul wasn't part of the program for this trip. But Ben couldn't get the guy out of his thoughts.

Abdul. That was the face of the guy in the YouTube production. The one who decapitated Nazmin. But they had no idea where Abdul was now. Moshe argued they needed good intel to set up the hit. In the black of night, the Humvees split up. Seven continued toward the border as Ben's and Moshe's peeled off to a rural area along the Indus River. Following the dirt road for several miles, Ben located the house where Rashida lived with a Pakistani man. Although both of them pretended to be a faithful married Muslim couple, they were collecting intel for Ben in the surrounding mosques, talking with local tribal leaders, filtering everything back to the Dark Horse Guardians.

His Humvee pulled around the backside of the house and Moshe's followed. Elvis rode with Ben, and would stand watch. They were expected by Rashida and her fictitious husband, Timur. The side door opened and Moshe followed Ben inside. Ben asked Elvis to stay hidden in the brush near the vehicles, listening, watching.

Only candlelight illuminated the room. Ben embraced Rashida and she smiled. Ben whispered, "We don't want to stay here long….it will put you in danger. I need you to help me with identifying someone ~ who is this guy?" Ben held his phone up with the gruesome YouTube video and stopped it midstream. He touched the photo and enlarged it. "His name is Abdul, but that's all we know."

Ben noticed the frightened stare Rashida shot at Timur. Then, she spoke, "We know him. He is the son of Salib Madi, the man who is the mastermind behind this reign of terror. Abdul is young, about twenty, I think. He's been to the mosque whipping up the young men into a frenzy, recruiting for his father. He bragged about that video. The people here have viewed it. They're frightened beyond what you can imagine. People are terrified to leave their homes or anger this Salib Madi in any way. They will be dragged out in the middle of the day to be tortured, beheaded, or set afire. I have photographs of Salib Madi's sons, Ibrahim, Abdul, and Saleh."

As she brought the photos upon the screen of her phone, Ben studied them in the candlelight. "Damn...*we had him*. This Abdul guy. He pretended he was deaf and mute. *We let him go*. He was visiting another target we took out. Damn it, Moshe....we let this guy go!" Ben slammed his fist upon the table awash with anger and frustration.

"It's too late now," Moshe muttered. "At least we know who the hell he is and what he looks like. We will get him, eventually."

"But he knows what we look like. He knows where we were. All of those friendlies will pay for their affiliation with us. We've got to kill the little bastard....like now." Ben insisted.

"It's not on our schedule. Besides, he didn't see that much. It's dangerous. We're on our way out," Moshe cautioned. "We can't get caught up with Abdul right now. We'll put it on the docket for next time."

"I'm staying." Ben stared at Rashida. "I'll hide by the river and lure him here somehow."

"Too dangerous." Moshe reiterated. "Come on. We're getting out of here."

"Wait." Rashida whispered. "They want you, Ben. There's a half million bounty for you. It's a well-known fact. Don't leave the way you came, just in case you've been followed. I have a good man on the river. His name is Wasem. He will bring you downstream in the night, no one will see you."

Moshe glanced at Ben nervously. "It's not in our plan."

"I'll do it. I need a little boat ride to get familiar with this terrain. I'm going to kill this bastard that murdered Nazmin. I want to be the one who kills him." Ben could feel the blood pulsing in his veins, rage building, adrenaline flowing. He knew it was dangerous to lose control, but he couldn't help the feelings coursing through him.

"What's the meeting point?" Moshe asked looking at the satellite map on his phone.

"Right there." Ben pointed to a dock about three miles south. "Call your man, Rashida, have him come for me."

Moshe and Elvis left with the Humvees and drove to the appointed site. Ben felt compelled to do this. But he was running on pure instinct. He left Rashida's house in the wee hours of the morning. No sunlight yet, but he could barely discern the outline of a man paddling a skiff toward him. Soundlessly, and with the precision of a cat, Ben allowed his body to spring into the air and land on the hard surface of the boat. He shook hands with Wasem. "Three miles down to the dock." Ben smiled. Wasem nodded and used a pole to push away from the shore.

Unknown to Moshe and Elvis, Ben felt the eyes of someone on him. Who it was, he wasn't certain, but Ben had a weapon, body armor, G's and his senses. Someone was watching him. The hackles remained. He watched for movement. With the help of the G's, he detected a man hidden on the riverbank. As the skiff glided soundlessly with the current downstream, they covered three miles in a short period of time. Wasem was a wealth of information. He knew Abdul and the places he would most likely be found. The mosque in Bhakkar was Abdul's comfort zone. This was what he needed to know.

As the skiff pulled up beside the dock, Ben's G's picked up a figure standing near a vehicle a good distance away in a dirt parking lot. The outline of the man barely moved, and Ben did not let on that he saw him. Wasem dropped him off and continued down the river. One of the Humvees pulled up and Ben hopped in. As they whisked by the parking lot, the figure crouched in the darkness.

"What the hell was that all about?" Elvis exhaled, his exasperation obvious.

"We're being followed. I just wanted to make sure." Ben answered.

"By who?" Elvis asked.

"I'm not sure. I wish I could stay and find out." Ben said with a tinge of frustration.

"You're like a dog on a chain, man. Cool down." Elvis sent a sidelong glance his way.

Ben took a deep breath and realized if he was being followed, he was observed going into Rashida's house. Not good. The same thing that happened to Nazmin could happen to her. This was his worst nightmare, putting those providing him intel into harm's way. Ben tapped his phone and Rashida's voice came on. "Get the hell out of there, now. You've been made. Someone was following me. I don't know who the hell it is yet, but I know there are two of them, working in conjunction. I'm concerned about your safety. One of the Humvees will double back and bring you and Timur with us back to Israel."

Although pumped with adrenaline to hunt down Nazmin's killer, Ben knew Moshe was right. His SEAL training taught him the same thing. His anger and rage would only serve to undermine him. The cooler head would always prevail. The Humvees made their way back to Israel. It was time to go home.

Chapter 11

Black Site in Northern Maine

~ Lara ~

Opening her eyes at daybreak in the steel hut to a crackling fire and the smell of bacon frying was not as bad as she had anticipated. Monique and Rusty were already awake, and taking turns using the rustic bathroom. She rolled over and closed her eyes for a moment and Einstein licked her face.

"Hey, buddy." Lara spoke softly and rubbed his soft bull-dog fur. She knew he needed to go outside, so she slipped on her coat, her Glock, and boots and walked into the kitchen.

"Breakfast is almost ready..." Alvin smiled. His lanky body leaned over the gas stove, as he tended to several pans simultaneously.

"Smells delicious." Lara smiled back at him. "I'll take the dog out for a moment."

Rusty was right behind her, "Not without me." He slipped on his coat, Glock and gloves, then unbolted the door. Stepping outside there was no sound, except for the scurrying of a few birds and a squirrel.

"Where the hell does he get bottled gas around here?" Lara asked.

"There's a guy we know..." Rusty smiled. "Don't worry. He's a prepper friend of ours. He helped us set this place up. We take care of him, he takes care of us."

"I'm worried, Rusty." Lara gazed into his eyes, searching for a sign of hope.

"I'm not," he assured her. "Nobody knows about this place. And, even if someone did try to do anything, we have enough guns and ammo to take out a mid-sized army. We will lay low for a few days here. I've been in touch with Captain Redman. I don't trust him completely. Just want you to know. He has no friggin' idea where we are."

"Yes, he's part of the bureaucracy, or should I say the politburo?" Lara could see her breath. "Damn, it's cold. Let's go back inside." Einstein was shivering, too.

The two scurried back to the warmth of the fire. It was time for breakfast and they ate heartily. Lara realized Alvin could have been a chef, if he wasn't a taxidermist and a black-site overseer. The man had skills. Not only that, he was friendly and intelligent. The chatter at the breakfast table made her feel normal for a moment. Afterwards, Alvin heated several kettles of water on the woodstove and poured it into the copper bathtub. "It's all yours, Lara."

He closed the door as she disrobed and slipped into the hot water submerging herself. She washed her hair and soaped from head to toe. For a few minutes, she allowed herself to relax.

When she emerged from the bath, Rusty tapped on the door. "It's Ben. He's on his way home. Just wanted you to know."

Lara's words caught in her throat, "Oh God, thank you." She quickly dressed and combed her wet hair. Ben had left word for them to meet him at a rest stop between Boston and Maine. It was an out-of-the-way sort of place. Lara, Rusty, and Monique got Einstein into the Jeep and said goodbye to Alvin.

"Ben's got some sort of plan." Rusty said. "Or he wouldn't be asking us to meet him."

"I have a feeling I know what he's going to do." Lara whispered.

"Yeah, me too." Rusty exhaled. "I'll help in any way that I can."

~ Ben ~

Once landing at Logan Airport, Ben sent a text to Rusty. If he had this figured out correctly, he timed their meeting to coincide perfectly. He rolled his gear to the shuttle bus and was back in his beat-up Nissan heading toward the meet site. All he could think about was protecting Lara and Monique from whomever was following them. Although the police were on the case, he had little faith that they'd follow through and catch the bastards. His plan was better.

Three hours later, in darkness, he arrived at the rest stop in Maine. It was not a well-known place. A traveler would have to get off at Exit 23 and the sign was not readily evident. This particular stop was in a well-wooded area with a circular dirt drive that lead up to an elevated spot. He liked this locale because of the great visibility. As he parked and hopped out of his vehicle, he spied the Jeep carrying the most precious cargo. Perfect timing.

The moment his eyes took in Lara, he ran to embrace her. She jumped into his arms and wrapped her legs around his waist. "Oh Ben…" he felt her whispering in his ear. As she kissed him, he felt Lara's tears soaking his face and tasted the salt as he kissed her willing mouth. She was saying, "I missed you…", but he could think of nothing but holding her, kissing her as a frenzied passion swept over him without warning. He needed her as a starving man needed bread. His mind was focused on her, and only her.

Einstein was pushing on his legs, rubbing against him, wanting to be greeted. But, he couldn't look down at the dog just yet. He could not release Lara from his arms, and he didn't want her to see the tears welling in his eyes. He was speechless for a moment and glad that she spoke first.

"Oh God, Ben, I missed you…" Lara choked on the words as he set her down. Monique and Rusty piled on and group-hugged him. He fell to his knees and roughed up Einstein's fur, as the dog whined with delight.

"I missed you, too." he whispered. He stood in the darkness facing them. "The whole Dark Horse team is staying at Clearwater Farm. We will take turns standing watch. We're getting intel on the guys following. We'll kill them. It's as simple as that. Let's go. Lara, you come with me and bring Einstein. Rusty, I'll meet you at the farm. The team is already there. They've gone over every inch of the place. There are detectives at the top of the driveway. Just tell them you're part of the guest list; they're expecting you."

Within a couple of minutes, he had Lara secured in a seatbelt in the front seat and Einstein wedged into the backseat with his gear. He leaned over to do what he had been dreaming of doing for the last ten days. Taking Lara's face into his hands, he touched his lips to hers, tasting the salty tears. "No more crying." He whispered, pulling her hair back. "It's all right. I'm here. Don't worry. Oh, darlin, I missed you so much...." He kissed her again and revved the engine. *She was revving his engine.* He realized the sooner he got on the road, the sooner he'd be in a hot shower with her.

The Nissan traveled at a high rate of speed to get to Clearwater Farm. The detectives waved him through, and it was then that Ben blew out a heavy sigh of relief. They unpacked the car and were inside by daybreak. Ben hugged his brothers and they slapped each other as if they hadn't seen one other for a long time, even though they had just spent the last ten days together. It was more of a celebration of life for a moment. Then the exhaustion kicked in.

Rusty and Gus volunteered to be first watch. The others all made their way to a guest bedroom.

Ben took Lara's hand and brought her to the master bedroom shower. He closed the door and scooped her into his arms. She snuggled against his chest. Whenever he pulled her into him this way and she melded to him, there was no doubt she belonged with him. They fit together perfectly. He wanted her close to his chest, close to his heart, always. "Oh, darlin, this is where I want to be, with you."

Ben's hands never left her. His fingers ran under her shirt and across her back, craving her soft skin, her feminine smell, her delicious mouth. His lips went to hers as if magnetically drawn. Although he was tired earlier, he felt a rush of adrenaline careening through him. As his rough hands caressed Lara's softness, his hormones went into overdrive.

It was as if the entire world melted away and the two of them were the only ones existing.

Nuzzling her neck, he moved his hand to her breast and lightly traced her nipple with his thumb. He felt her respond, and knew she wanted him as much as he wanted her. She was placing light kisses on his face, neck and chest, driving him mad with anticipation. A feeling of uncontrollable joy flooded through him. How could he live without her every day, every night? It was getting more difficult. He fought off enemies, but he now wanted Lara to overthrow him. She probably didn't know she had complete power over him, something he had never experienced before. As her hands and lips continued on the hungry search of his body, he laid back. Just watching her caress him, brought him to a height of arousal that was uncontrollable.

"Oh, don't stop," he whispered. "I can't take another day without you, without this. I love you so much, darlin."

"You're here and you're mine, right now," she murmured between kisses. "I'm not letting you go. I've been dreaming of you."

"Don't, baby. Don't let me go." Ben felt himself saying. He waited while she undressed him, but he helped her along. The eagerness could not be stopped or delayed. He wanted her so badly, he felt an ache inside that wouldn't stop. He inhaled the sweet clean scent of her hair and tugged at her clothing. His heart was pounding non-stop, as he imagined all of the ways in which he could please her. Her full soft lips were on his mouth and the sensation was driving him wild. Kissing her was a delight unto itself; her velvety lips parted and her tongue invited his in.

Her hands held his face, unshaven and disheveled, and she gazed into his eyes with pure love. "I want to make you feel good, Ben, I have missed you so much. I want…" He placed his finger on her lips and she took it into her mouth. He felt her sucking on his finger and her eyes locked with his. Damn. She could kiss his finger and drive him wild. What guy in his right mind would walk away from this, willingly? He had to be some kind of idiot.

~ Lara ~

Taking a hot shower together, she felt as if she was having the most beautiful dream. Ben was with her in the shower, kissing her, washing her hair and holding her as if he couldn't let her go. She knew he was exhausted, but he was ready for lovemaking. And, as tired as she was, she wanted him more than ever.

As they toweled one another off, she felt impulsive. She let herself feel happiness, then giggled, "Where have you been?"

"That's top secret, ma'am…" Ben said in a stern voice. Her back was against the bathroom wall, and he was above her covering her mouth with his. She felt his tongue probing. Judging from his urgent French kiss, she sensed there would be no restraint. But, surprising her, he took a deep breath and brought her hand to his mouth. Kissing the palm of her hand, he whispered, "I want you, darlin. I'll do my best to take my time."

"Just love me, Ben. I can't wait either. Do whatever you want. I missed you so much." She spoke the words, thinking she sounded bold. All she knew was: she wanted him, and couldn't slow her own arousal. Longing, yearning, whatever it was – it was strong. It was more than yearning, it was an ache that wouldn't go away. She had played this out in her mind so many times lying in bed alone.

Tugging him by the hand, she insisted he recline upon the bed, and she sat atop him. She let her wet dark hair surround her, and felt his hands reaching for her face. His strong arms pulled her onto him. His kiss was urgent, warm and wet. He was an expert at French-kissing, while his hands skimmed her waist and outer thighs, then moved to her rear. She felt his hard erection against her belly. *Oh – this was going to be a delightful treat.*

His hands grasped her bottom with an urgency, but she arched her back slightly and he suckled her breast. Frantic for one long moment, she wanted to tease him, savor everything about him. Although she was on top, in control, there were times when she really wasn't. His mouth on her nipple shot a wave of electricity through her, making her want to relinquish any semblance of power. She wanted him to linger with her erect nipples for a while, a sweet sensual pleasure.

Lara slipped her hand between his legs and grabbed his throbbing hardness. At that moment, it felt as if a switch had been thrown. She suddenly became even more eager to please him, but also wanted more than ever to enjoy the most intimate part of her handsome husband. She could hear his breathing quicken as she moved lower; he grew harder and his breath caught in his throat. She watched him through half-closed eyes as a slow, secret smile came over his lips. His eyes met hers momentarily, then closed.

Stroking him, she watched as his body responded involuntarily. Incredibly sexy, she watched his manhood glisten in the sunlight filtering through the drapes. She could no longer stop herself from wanting him – all of him. Mounting him, she heard him exhale and she put her hands on his muscled chest. She began moving him against her, so that he was at the entrance of her warm, wet spot. Swollen and ready, she gasped as his erection slid inside. She ceased moving for a moment and clenched him, instinctively knowing he was feeling pure pleasure. She heard him cry out. Then, slowly, methodically, she moved up and down, writhing in pleasure as waves of ecstasy overtook her.

~ Ben ~

It was as if Lara could read his mind. She was doing all of the things he wanted, touching him in a way that drove him wild. Watching her gyrate on him, he was captivated. Lovemaking with her was incredible. She leaned down to touch his chest, and he felt her lips on him, everywhere. Her mouth was tantalizing, and made him frantic to the point of not knowing if he wanted them on his mouth, his chest, or his cock. Damn, he wanted her to kiss him everywhere all at once.

When she pulled him inside of her, he had no restraint left. She was in control, and he enjoyed the show. He suspected she had no idea how sexy she looked moving on him that way, how she felt sliding against his body. He traced her mouth with his thumb and she sucked his finger. A moment later she kissed his chest, then her lips were on his mouth and she was wildly panting, thrilling him to the point of no return. As she rode him rhythmically, the sensation became a sensual grinding movement, lasting much longer than he thought it would. Carnal pleasure overwhelmed him as he completely lost control. He cried out with delight as she drove him wild.

Exhausted, she collapsed upon him, her face next to his. He felt her breathing erratically, while he fought to control his own ragged breath. "Don't think you're done," he whispered. After a few moments, he felt her body relax, and her face turned to his. He kissed her forehead as she nuzzled against his chest. He enjoyed the warmth of her body against him, and pulled the sheet and blanket over them creating a comfortable cocoon. Illuminated by a sliver of sunlight, her beautiful face, was the last image he recalled before falling into deep slumber.

~ Abdul ~

He had been in touch with the Americans, Aaron and Tim. But, somehow, Lara Keegan managed to elude them. They had followed her Mercedes in the night through New Hampshire, into Massachusetts, then they lost her. They were searching for Lara, but no sign of her had surfaced yet.

The Muslim Fellowship leaked the information as requested by the CIA Director. The Muslim Fellowship was now in the State Department, as well as the Department of Homeland Security, and the Department of Defense, and the Muslim Fellowship was at Abdul's beck and call.

Abdul knew it would only be a matter of time before they'd be able to stop Keegan, and all of the CIA snooping on his fellow jihadists. The group had even infiltrated the FBI and the CIA. It would be discrimination for them to be turned down for these government jobs. Abdul loved the liberal legal system in the United States of America. It was ripe for infiltration, and would be easy to take over with Sharia Law, little by little. Death by a thousand cuts. Stealth jihad.

Sharia law was already being implemented in New Jersey, Texas, Florida, Canada, and had a stronghold in Michigan. Every day, orders were being given by his father on Twitter, with lists of American soldiers to kill, complete with names and addresses. The terror cell used Google maps to locate their targets. His brothers were more than happy to sacrifice their lives in order to kill as many American soldiers as possible. Each one killed was a credit to their cause and martyrdom was their calling.

The Muslim Fellowship was now actively promoting gun control, collecting millions of dollars for the cause of making America a gun-free zone. *And, it was working.* Entire states, like New York and even the capitol of the nation, banned gun ownership, and made very few exceptions. Government buildings, public schools, campuses at universities, and entire large cities were now soft targets. Their precious Second Amendment was being eroded, little by little. But, the Muslim

Fellowship had a great deal of patience, money, and influence. Soon, all of America would be a gun-free zone, making Islamic take-over free of resistance.

Co-existing with the infidel was ideal. They even sold bumper stickers to further their cause. They were lulling the Americans into a sense of fellowship, peace, security. The Americans were too busy watching sports and entertaining themselves with recreational drugs to be aware of what was really taking place in their country. Good. Go to the movies, enjoy your free time. Argue over the sporting competitions. Go to the casino. Abdul was happy that those he wished to bring to submission would be so easy to subdue. They were fat, lazy and ignorant. And, soon they'd be unarmed. Perfect for overthrowing when the time was right.

Even though most of the plans the Muslim Fellowship had made were coming to fruition, he still hadn't captured Keegan. His father, the great Salib Madi, was ranting and raving today, even though Abdul had managed to be captured, then released by this Keegan. He thought his father would sing his praises for being so clever, for pretending to be a deaf mute and escaping. *But, it was exactly the opposite. His father was angry, more so now than ever.*

Thus, Ibrahim and Abdul had come up with the perfect plan to kill Keegan. It might take weeks, months, even a year, because Keegan already knew they were searching for him. Keegan managed to secure his family in his Clearwater Farm safe house. But, how long could he remain safe from the hunting party that would be tracking him every minute of every day? Abdul smiled as he read the latest intel on his laptop. Keegan was feeling pretty protected. He left his compound at least once a day. Tracking his movements, Aaron and Tim fed him information. Once he and Ibrahim got to the United States and made their own observations, things would progress more rapidly.

The knock on the door jolted him out of his reverie of killing Ben Keegan. Abdul knew it was Saleh, his half-brother, although he seldom admitted to it. Although lately, Saleh was surprising him. Just the other day, Saleh had cut Ibrahim's face with a fixed blade in a fight. Ibrahim's pride was still wounded, but his face was healing well. Saleh seemed to be coming into his manhood, standing up for himself more. These were good qualities for an Islamic soldier.

Saleh cracked the door after knocking, "Did you say to come in?"

"Yes." Abdul gestured for him to sit. He liked the way Saleh deferred to him; it showed he respected power, another good trait for a jihadist to have. Maybe Saleh could be useful after all.

"How can I help you?" Saleh asked him, with a little bit of defiance in his black eyes. He looked much more like his mother than his father. But, that was fine with him. Abdul was glad he looked like his father more than any of his half-brothers. They envied him because he got preferential treatment due to the resemblance. It was rumored his father wanted Abdul to be the top general in the army of the Islamic State. If he brought Ben Keegan's head to him, it would surely elevate him to the highest position. He wanted nothing more.

"We are going to America. We have the visa paperwork prepared for you because you had mentioned you wanted to help us kill Ben Keegan. Do you want to go?" Abdul asked.

"Yes, of course, where do I sign?" Saleh responded eagerly. Good. He was ready to do this.

"You, me, and Ibrahim, will all be college students. We are going to the United States on a student visa. Not to worry about attending classes or anything like that. We will be free to roam once we get there. But, we will sign up for classes and attend just enough to look like we are students. Do you understand?" Abdul exhaled.

"Yes." Saleh eagerly signed the paperwork and pushed it across the desk. "When do we leave?"

"Tomorrow I knew you'd sign the visa paperwork and want to go with us. Lately, you have been eager to help. So, I purchased plane tickets. We will fly together, the three of us." Abdul extended the ticket envelope to Saleh. As he reached to take it, Abdul pulled it away. He watched Saleh's eyes as he experienced confusion, then defiance once again.

"What's the matter?" Saleh asked, staring into his eyes.

"Here, take them." Abdul handed the tickets to him. "I just want you to know, I can take things away as quickly as I give them. Don't forget that, Saleh…."

"I won't," Saleh said, still making eye contact, looking defiant.

"Make sure you don't forget." Abdul wanted to have the last word, and he did, as Saleh slinked out of the room.

Chapter 12

~ Lara ~

Living in lockdown for the past two months with Ben and his brotherhood settled into a comfortable routine, and she never believed she could enjoy having so many people at her house for an extended period of time. She began to feel they were her family. Together, the group worked with precision toward one goal: survival. Even though they were being stalked, when inside and sharing dinner or telling stories, it seemed like one big camping trip.

Everyone worked together and they learned from one another. The men stood watch around the clock and made trips to the grocery store. The women home-schooled the children at Clearwater Farm. Lara was getting to know each Dark Horse Guardian personally. She loved the men as if they were her own brothers. Each one had a unique personality and brought special gifts to the table.

But, more importantly, for the first time in her life she really bonded with women in a way she had never done before. The women married to these unique men fascinated Lara and taught her more than she ever could've imagined. They were strong, confident, capable, and above all, dedicated to their families. Even though the atmosphere at her quiet seaside manor could be overwhelming at times, Lara would not have missed this for the world. She learned as much from the women as the men. The unique challenge was keeping the children from becoming bored during the winter months of January, February, and March.

Ben continued teaching at the university part-time, and security was ramped up there, as well. The board of directors at the university were more than happy to do it, due to the fact that there had been an increase in campus crime in the last year anyway. Plus, Ben offered to pay for the extra security. He employed a few more veterans returning from the Middle East -- guys he knew and trusted.

It drove some of the anti-gun advocates on campus a little crazy to have the armed personnel there, but the security detail blended in. You'd never know they were former Navy SEALs.

But Lara knew -- if someone wanted to kill a person, having extra security would not necessarily prevent it. And, she constantly worried about what might happen next. She had deep concerns about losing Ben to a well-aimed bullet, or any of the others, for that matter. She had grown to love this extended family much more than she could have imagined.

Her friendship with Monique deepened, as well. It was a wonderful diversion when she and Monique left to do design work at the bungalow. Often Rusty or Bettencourt would go along with them, plus Lara carried her firearm religiously. Lately, business had taken off. Home renovations were trending in favor of moving.

"I wonder when we will be able to move about freely and not be afraid." Monique asked as they rode in a different vehicle every day. Today it was an older Chevy Suburban with peeling paint and a dent or two, but it was fitted with bullet-proof windows and plating.

"I don't know " Lara stared out of the window watching the outside world go by, remembering there was once a time when she was in the driver's seat.

The problem, Lara knew, wasn't Madi's men. It was the next million after him who were the problem. With Ben's cover blown, he and Lara would have a target on their backs for their rest of their natural lives. From that day forward, they were one bullet away from planning their own funerals, or several funerals, for that matter. This was the one constant worry cycling through her mind day and night.

As they waited in the parking lot, Bettencourt went inside the bungalow, checking to make sure all was well. He spoke on the com and told them to come inside.

"I'll make coffee." Lara volunteered. She went into the kitchen and noticed something was not right. The cupboards had been opened and several items were askew, including the coffee maker.

"What's up?" Bettencourt said, leaning against the kitchen door casing.

"Nothing much. Just some things seem messed up here." Lara said.

"Like what?" Bettencourt asked. "Give me details."

Lara showed him, and he spoke on his com to Rusty, "Look around. See if it looks like someone might have been here….stuff in the kitchen has been messed with…"

Lara watched Bettencourt as he went through every square inch of the tiny kitchen looking for anything he could find. He took a plastic bag from the drawer and used two toothpicks to pick up a few items and put them into the baggie.

"What was that all about?" Lara quizzed him.

"Just some fresh mud and a couple of other things. I have a feeling someone has been in here, but they didn't want us to know." Bettencourt gazed into her eyes, all business-like. "You know what that means…"

Lara's eyes locked with his. "We'll not be able to work here any longer."

"Yup." Bettencourt exhaled. He waved to Monique and asked her to help pack up everything they needed. They were heading back to the farm. Lara's heart sank. She knew what was coming, more restrictions, with more lockdown time. There was only one way to end this. It would be violent, but necessary.

~ Abdul ~

The student visa idea was a good one. The three men were now in an apartment near the campus where Ben Keegan was teaching. Ibrahim followed Keegan on a regular basis, and some days he followed his wife, Lara.

"What did you find in the bungalow the other day?" Abdul questioned Ibrahim.

"Nothing, really...it was a waste of time. There were some items in the kitchen. It looks like they work or eat there on a regular basis." Ibrahim reported.

"Good. We could place some C4 there and detonate when she's there."

Then his attention turned to Saleh. "How about you? What have you found out about the layout of Clearwater Farm?" Abdul asked pointedly.

"Here's the map from city hall. I told them my father is looking at purchasing an adjoining property. They gave me this information willingly. I flew a drone over the place and captured this video. Here, I will send it to you on your phone, if you'd like." Saleh offered.

"No, keep it on your phone. I can watch it there." Abdul commanded. After viewing the footage, he had to admit, he hadn't thought of buying a hobby drone and flying over Keegan's property. The thought might have come to him later, but Saleh was proving to be very helpful and useful. Maybe he had underestimated him all along.

~ Saleh ~

Feeding information to Ben Keegan was the biggest challenge for Saleh. For one thing, his cell phone was not secure. Abdul frequently looked at his iPhone. Keegan had supplied him with a burner phone, which he used. He tucked it into the band of his underwear. All of his communication with Keegan was done via encrypted texts and e-mails. No talking. Keegan had explained there were too many ears and eyes in the United States regarding phone calls. They were all recorded, whether they needed to be or not. The encrypted texts and e-mails would be a better idea. But, Saleh was nervous that somehow Abdul would find the burner phone. Even if he did, the words on it were encrypted. Nevertheless, Saleh still had nightmares about it sometimes.

Today, Saleh was going to the far end of the parking lot to send a message to Keegan, letting him know about the drone footage and about Ibrahim's breaking into the bungalow. He hadn't known Ibrahim was going to do that. Saleh tried to get the women and children out of the picture. He attempted to focus Abdul and Ibrahim on their prime target, Ben Keegan. But they often argued it would be best to capture a family member, and then they could get Keegan. Their focus was Lara.

The text today was critical. Abdul was bringing another terrorist to the United States to help with the mission. The new guy had a reputation for going off on his own. He had a big ego, was unpredictable and had killed many Christians -- innocent women and children, posing for pictures with their dead mangled bodies and posting the photos on social media.

Right now, it was Abdul, Ibrahim, Saleh, Aaron and Tim. But, this guy was only known as Khouri. Saleh had little information about him, except he was a wild one. Saleh told Ben in the text, once Khouri arrived, he'd let him know as much as possible. He did hear today from Abdul that they could not return to Pakistan until Keegan was dead or captured. Their father was on a rampage. He was grasping at straws, trying to kill Ben Keegan. It was his major topic of conversation. He had become obsessed with killing Keegan.

~ Ben ~

Being home with Lara the last few months had been nerve-wracking for him. It was as if he was on a mission and he had her with him to protect at all times. The Dark Horse Guardians were in a state of upheaval, but acted with professionalism and precision. Even though their families were stuck on the compound of Clearwater Farm, they made the best of it. And, he noticed Lara was bonding with each person on his team. There was some good coming of this awful situation.

But Ben could tell Lara was sometimes exhausted having that many people around all day and all night. Their private life was no longer private. One time a child walked into their master bedroom while they were making love. Of course, he laughed it off, but Lara wasn't too happy about it.

Then there was mealtime and bedtime every night, filled with routines and rituals that seemed to intrude on his and Lara's personal time together. Lara always ended up helping one of the women with an unruly or sick child. She was kind, hard-working, and generous, however, and he often wondered how she put up with him and all that was taking place. She took it in stride and smiled.

When she returned home from her design work in the late afternoon today, he would walk with her on the beach and kiss her, hoping for a tiny sliver of privacy. Soon it would be their one-year wedding anniversary. Monique and Bettencourt were planning their wedding. They wanted to have it at Clearwater Farm, but it was on lockdown at the moment. It seemed all of their lives were on hold.

The April sun was warmer now, and Lara would often walk with him after dinner for a short while with Einstein, just like when things were normal. But things weren't normal, and he wanted more than ever to get back to a semblance of their old routine. Hopefully, Saleh would help him get there.

He saw the Suburban coming down the driveway and knew Lara was in it. Einstein did, too. The dog whined with excitement. As Monique, Lara, Bettencourt, and Rusty exited the vehicle, within seconds, there was gun fire. Not knowing the direction it was coming from, Bettencourt instructed Lara and Monique to stay in the vehicle, as he drew his weapon. Rusty and Lara did the same, automatically taking cover. The vehicle had been bullet-proofed, but they instinctively crouched as another round hit the Suburban. The bullet lodged in the backside of the vehicle. Then, more rounds hit it, all coming from the same direction. Bettencourt spoke into his com, "It's a lone gunman. Got his location, south cliff."

Ben watched as Bettencourt took aim with his H&K M23. The big man crouched near the edge of the vehicle, took careful aim, and got off ten rapid rounds in the direction of the ledge.

Gus and Tom were already awake inside. Ben spoke on the com, "Get the Silver Shadows, we're going to play laser tag from the upstairs windows."

It wasn't long before Ben realized this wasn't the greatest spot to be pinned down under gunfire. There were rocky bluffs surrounding them and long stretches of sandy beach. Not a lot of cover, except for the house, itself. The windows were hurricane-proof, but he didn't think they'd stop a bullet and didn't want to test them right now. He dreaded the thought of bullets going into the house, killing someone randomly. He spoke into the com, "Get everyone down to the basement in the middle of the house, now!"

Crouching on the porch yielding his Glock, more bullets came toward Ben, one whizzed right by his head. He held his breath for a moment. The next bullet caught him in the left shoulder. He winced and cried out in pain as it grazed through his clothing.

"Shit. He breathed into his com. "Damn it -- I caught a bullet in my shoulder."

Ben trained his 9mm Glock19 on the south cliff and fired twelve rounds. Within the course of two minutes, Ben heard the Silver Shadow let go above him, and the distinct sound of a bullet hitting its mark. Thud, thud, thud. The small cannon with a laser scope painted its target, as Gus dropped one guy from the cliff. They frantically searched for any others, but Ben surmised they scurried away as the police siren grew louder in the distance.

Ben waited under cover until the police arrived. Once the area was secured, the Dark Horse Guardians emerged. The police examined the body. "He's a young man by the name of Aaron Brown. We know him; there's a warrant out for his arrest. We think he might have killed Officer Simpson." the police officer spoke matter-of-factly. "This guy has been in and out of trouble for a while. Well, he won't be bothering you any longer. Hey, you're bleeding. We'll get a medic here to take a look at that."

Ben sat down in the kitchen feeling defeated. "Yeah. Thanks. But, we've got it covered." Elvis got the medical kit and pulled Ben's jacket off, then his shirt.

"Yeah, that'll leave a mark." He teased Ben.

"Screw you, too." Ben smiled, then winced as Elvis meticulously cleaned the gash in his shoulder.

~ Lara ~

Fawning over Ben's bullet grazing wasn't the thing to do; she found that out the hard way. Ben pretended it wasn't much more than a mosquito bite, in fact those were his words. The men in the kitchen were laughing, as if it was no big deal. Having seen the scars on his body, she suddenly realized it wasn't much compared to some of the others. But she winced thinking it had to hurt. The fact that it even happened heightened her sense of worry, not only regarding Ben, but all of them corralled at the compound right now.

"No drama, darlin," Ben whispered after he was bandaged. He kissed her forehead sweetly, but she could see his demeanor was serious. As far as Ben was concerned, the incident was one of many. But for Lara, she imagined all of the catastrophic things that could've happened in that split second.

Interrupting her apprehension, she scooped up two crying children. Dinner was being prepared late, and the police warned them about stepping outside for any length of time. Lara was gravely concerned about the shooting. How did Aaron Brown get that close to the compound? The security system would have gone off to alert them. But, her answer came minutes later. Ben noticed that somehow, someone had messed with the security camera that was covering that side of the compound, and the alarm didn't go off. He resynched it, and all was fine. But he still wanted to get to the bottom of why it malfunctioned. And she knew he would.

Aaron Brown was dead. Lara was so angry, she wished she could've been the one to shoot him, but it was Gus who got off the lucky shot. She felt fortunate that the dead man was a terrorist, and not her husband.

Instead of getting involved in the police processing, she sat in the weapons cache room and went over the fine points of using a Silver Shadow, the weapon Ben's team preferred. It performed perfectly in the execution of Aaron Brown. She pulled the double barreled AR15 up and studied the weapon closely. Rusty was organizing weapons and ammo in the room silently.

"It's made in Israel..." she whispered.

"Like what you see?" Rusty turned toward her. "It's a thing of beauty. It has the same precision guided tag and shoot technology found in fighter jets."

"Yes, I love it." Lara felt herself becoming engrossed with the unique firearm, admiring its qualities, and quickly understanding why the Dark Horse Guardians preferred it. "I want one."

"And you know the rule: no guns until I can take you to the range and teach you how to use it. Each one is different." Rusty reiterated. "This is a serious piece of firepower."

"I like the stainless steel barrel, what's the advantage of that?" Lara queried.

"Accuracy is truer, plus it doesn't overheat so easily if you're popping off a lot of rounds." Rusty said.

For a moment, it felt as if they were on the pond at Rusty's range, rambling on about a gun, as they'd done a hundred times before. But, right now, Lara realized their lives had been irrevocably changed. If there was ever a time when she wanted to help Ben, it was now. A plan started forming in her mind; an outrageous one, but it just might work.

"I've got something to discuss with you...." Lara started. "I know this sounds crazy, but I've been thinking of a way to end this whole thing quickly."

"I'm all ears..." Rusty smiled.

When she had finished explaining her idea, Rusty grinned from ear to ear. "Where the hell do you come up with this stuff?"

"You think I'm crazy...." Lara exhaled.

"No, I think it's brilliant. But, I've got to get Ben and the other guys on board. Let me handle this." Rusty put his arm around her shoulder. "It's actually possible, your scheme, but we've got to be careful."

Chapter 13

~ Ben ~

On the face of it, Lara's plan sounded a bit unpredictable, but the more he discussed it with the team, the better they liked it. Sure, it was fraught with uncertainty and possible problems, but they could use the Dark Horse Game to help them weed out the worst scenario, then the next, and go from there.

His phone vibrated and he recognized the Special Activities Director's ringtone and answered.

"Ben, I understand things are going badly there. I want to do everything I can to help." Kip Larson breathed into the phone.

"I've got this." Ben held his breath. He didn't want to give one morsel of information to Larson about what the team was planning.

"We can send in some special agents to help...." Larson offered. "The CIA cares about your family."

"No, really. Things are fine. I appreciate your offer. But, we are doing all right," Ben said calmly. Inside, he was envisioning his hands around Larson's neck. The leak that started all of this came from the State Department, and if he had to spend the rest of his life, he'd get the name of the bastard that was responsible for the leak. He prided himself on being able to find anyone at any time. If whoever did this thought he could hide behind a vanishing IP address; he was foolish to think that would give him anonymity. It might work with his little hacker pals, but not with him. Ben coded an app for that, too. Technically, there wasn't anyone, anywhere in the world that he couldn't find and kill. And, eventually, this State Department employee would be in his crosshairs; it didn't matter *where* he was. By committing the act of treason, the bastard painted a bull's eye on his own back. Leaking Ben's personal information, he painted a bull's eye right between his eyes.

Finally, Larson acquiesced and hung up. Good. It was time to do what needed to be done. First things first. Lara needed training on the Silver Shadow. It was an amazing weapon, but had to be handled nimbly and with care. Rusty thought it would be best to set up a firing range right there on the compound at Clearwater Farm. So, at night, the men set about building one on the beach.

Out of nowhere, several other former SEALs in the area offered their help. Ben welcomed them to the group as they joined the team for participation in the plan. The more eyes watching, the better. At their makeshift firing range, within two weeks Lara and Monique were hitting their marks with great accuracy. They could strip the weapon down and put it back together. The perimeter of the property was now reinforced with six more former SEALs and a few army rangers and a couple of marines; friends from the roadhouse. Lara insisted on paying them a generous salary for their hard work and dedication. Ben sensed she was eager to swing into action with the team, but he wasn't ready just yet. The next step was simulation for a few days in the gaming room.

For the next few weeks, Lara and Monique enjoyed designing for clients at home in Ben's office, when they weren't at shooting practice or helping out with childcare. At night, when the children were sleeping, Ben's office converted into the Dark Horse situation room. All of the team members logged into new computer stations Ben had installed and their work was laid before them. Lara and Monique wanted to participate, actually insisted upon it. The team no longer had any reservations. A well-placed bullet, center mass was all they needed. There was no difference if it came from a female or a male, as long as it hit its mark, the shot would be celebrated with gusto.

"We need to lure them here." Ben explained. "The situation needs to look real."

Bettencourt thought aloud, "We can set that beach scene up. But, I want the women and children out of the picture. Far out of the picture. How do you plan to do that?"

"She's thought of that, too," Ben smiled, "I'm provisioning the sailboat, little by little. I will take the women and children away in that. There's an island just off the coast, Fort Gorges. The U.S. Army Corps of Engineers put the fort on Hog Island Ledge, which is the entrance to the harbor of Portland, right around 1865. It is similar in size and construction to Fort Sumter, but is constructed of granite instead of brick. You can actually see it from here."

Ben showed photos of the fort on the big screen. "Fort Gorges was last used by the Army during World War II for storage of submarine mines. Accessing the island involves crossing areas with strong tidal currents and should only be attempted by Navy SEALs under the right conditions, using a proper boat, which I have."

"So, the women and children will be on an island that is basically an old fort?" Elvis asked.

"Yes, Einstein will be there, too." Ben stated. "As for the beach scene, we need Geminoid automatons that look exactly like us. We will dress them in our clothing, build a bonfire on the beach, play some music in the early evening.....and that will be the lure. They'll think we've dropped our guard. It will appear that we're having a celebration on a warm spring evening."

"The perimeter needs to be wider and reinforced." Gus noted.

"Yes. And, it will be. We will put the additional SEALs here, here, and here. Rangers will be on the east side, the marines on the west. Plenty of silver shadows for all of you. A huge shipment just arrived from Israel, courtesy of Moshe." Ben smiled.

But he felt the smile disappear as he continued, "The biggest problem will be avoiding our own bullets. The way this place is set up, we'll be fighting in a bowl. It's important we take the high ground, use the G's, and watch them come in. But, the moment the first shot goes off, they'll know our positions. We also don't know how many of them will come. Right now, my intel gives me four, maybe five. But, if it is more than that, we could be in for trouble. These bastards have access to the best weaponry. From what I've learned, some of the stuff Americans left behind in Iraq is now being utilized by them. It will be a night fight, so that will add an element, too. We're best at night, but if they have night vision goggles – it will level the playing field, a little, anyway."

The room fell silent. Ben could sense the team was thinking. Some of the men asked questions, others wanted to dive into the game, which would play out all of the different possibilities. After two hours of running through each scenario the artificial intelligence could throw at them, it was obvious they could be in a tough spot, unless it all came together without a hitch. But, Ben knew that was a rare thing. Every mission, no matter how well planned, always had unexpected events that seemed to occur at the most inopportune moment.

Rusty immediately went to work to obtain Geminoid automatons from Japan that would be suitable. Not an easy task, Ben knew. But, if anyone could do it, Rusty could. He was a magician, at times.

~ Abdul ~

Frustrated by Keegan's latest move, Abdul paced the floor of the living room in what he considered a second rate apartment. He wanted a more luxurious flat, but his father said that would attract too much attention. Lately, he had brought his father nothing but disappointment. In silence, Abdul replayed the events of the last few weeks. In discussing the execution of Keegan, one of the American men went off on his own and pulled the trigger. This was not something he had ordered, it just happened. Aaron Brown was a hothead. The whole incident was an embarrassment, his father had explained angrily on the phone. Abdul was blamed for having this incompetent idiot, Aaron Brown, affiliated with him. His father's anger was palpable. Salib Madi said the actions of this one man proved that Abdul as not a leader.

The noise at the door jarred him from his reflections. The rest of the jihadi cell arrived for the meeting. Ibrahim, Saleh, Tim and Khouri. Abdul had preconceived concerns about Khouri. He was forced to take him on due to his father's insistence. Khouri could be really good at scouting and killing, or an uncontrollable wild card, from what he had heard. He hoped he was wrong about the latter. But only time would tell. His father explained to Abdul, part of being a leader is controlling the actions of those you lead. Thus, he knew from the beginning, he had to take control of Khouri. This was his last chance.

As the men settled in the living room, Abdul began talking. "We have been watching Keegan for months now. One of our operatives, Aaron Brown, was killed because of his stupidity. He was spying on Keegan and decided to take a shot at him. Big mistake. Keegan has his team of Navy SEALs there and other reinforcements. We need to watch him around the clock. Don't do anything stupid like Brown did, or the same thing will happen to you." Abdul tried to sound like the leader his father expected him to be.

Not a good sign, Immediately, Khouri questioned his authority. "But, if I have a good shot at this Keegan, shouldn't I take him down? There's a half million bounty on his head. Why shouldn't I get it?"

Abdul stared into Khouri's dark and brooding eyes, hoping he had enough intimidation to give him pause. "No, that's exactly how you will get killed. Our approach here must be calculated. We need to exercise patience....do you know the meaning of that word, Khouri?" Already, Abdul suspected Khouri was only interested in obtaining the half million bounty and making a name for himself.

"Of course. My English is perfect. I don't understand your cowardice, however."

"I'm in charge of this operation; that's all you need to know," Abdul spoke loudly, swallowing the rage building inside of him. "Here is the plan. We watch the compound around the clock, night and day. I will bring more men, if needed. But, we must figure out Keegan's patterns, his comings and goings, hack his phone, his computers, lay low until the right moment. And, there will be a right moment. But, only I will be the one to determine that. No one else."

The room fell silent except for the ticking of the clock on the wall, which was beginning to drive Abdul crazy. It seemed the minutes and hours were ticking by, as his father screamed at him on the phone, daily now. Talking about the killing of Keegan, but yet not speaking about it. They knew all of their communications were monitored by the NSA and the U.S. government. But their moles in the NSA and Homeland Security were monitoring Keegan, too. And, Abdul had frequent face-to-face contacts who told him everything. They were friendly well-educated Muslims supportive to his cause, working for the NSA and selling him intelligence. Valuable information.

The third week of May was coming to an end, and he was no closer to executing Keegan than he was the day he arrived. His intelligence, however, had an interesting nugget of information in it today. Keegan was planning an outdoor barbeque with his fellow warriors on the beach at his house. He must be feeling fairly comfortable, if he was scheduling such a vulnerable affair. But, Abdul, being the cynic that he was, waited for further confirmation of this event Keegan was setting up. He wanted more proof that it was truly going to happen. But in the next day or two, the chatter confirmed it. Abdul began feeling hopeful for the first time since he'd arrived in the United States.

Ibrahim and Tim were watching the road going into Keegan's residence. Sure enough, trucks carrying food products and outside furnishings drove in and dropped off items for his Memorial Day celebration. Phone calls were intercepted saying to bring the family and other friends, they had food for everyone. *But, why would Keegan be in such a happy mood?* Memorial Day, it was a day to honor the dead. But, Keegan didn't seem to realize he'd be among them. Could he really be this foolish? Something didn't seem right....but, Abdul ordered the men to watch and wait. The date was fast approaching.

Chapter 14

Family dinners were large at Clearwater Farm with all of the extra mouths to feed. Over the past couple of months, the team and their family members became very close to Lara. She filled in as a school teacher, babysitter, nurse and story teller, when needed. The children had grown fond of her and she genuinely enjoyed expressing her inner child when with them. She knew their preferences and personal quirks. And, occasionally, she even fantasized about having a child with Ben. But, what a lifestyle to bring a child into. Black-ops. She never knew whether Ben would come home injured or even alive. The upheaval was similar to that of a military family, except now they had terrorists gunning for them. She dismissed the idea of getting pregnant any time in the near future. This was something she'd need to talk with Ben about if she could ever get him alone.

Meanwhile, Lara trained with the Silver Shadow diligently at the shooting range built in the back of the house behind the garden. It was off limits for the children, but she and Monique and Rusty spent hours in there. The place was filled with smoke when they were done, but Lara loved the smell of spent ammunition. The hot molten aroma became familiar to her, as well as the feeling of shooting the double barreled AR.

More than ever, she wanted to shoot outside. The weather had become warm and balmy. But, it was too dangerous to linger in the yard. They never knew who might be watching. The children had been amazingly well-behaved under the circumstances. They played games and stayed inside. The entire basement of Clearwater Farm had been turned into a giant playroom, sectioned off by age groups. One area had mats for tumbling and wrestling. Lara would often join the older children showing them basic self-defense moves and the holds Ben had taught her.

Today she sat alone with Monique, as Rusty cleaned up the spent ammo at the gun range.

"I'm ready to kill these guys….do you think you can do it?" Lara asked Monique point blank.

"Yes. I have had enough of this. I wouldn't hesitate." Monique seemed deadly serious.

"You can't hesitate." Rusty added. "If they are shooting at you, there's no time for hesitation. Just shoot."

Rusty finished and approached them, "One more thing, Lara. You and Monique will be protecting the women and children, as well as yourselves. You understand these terrorists could very well follow you to the fort and come after you. You have to be ready for that, if it happens."

Lara was well aware of the possibilities. She'd been in the Dark Horse game many times and that very scene played out before her in high resolution 3D. Every time it did, she imagined pulling the trigger on the Silver Shadow killing as many of them as she could with rapid fire.

She turned to Rusty, "Has all of the equipment been delivered for the beach party? And, the other stuff?"

"Yes," Rusty answered. "We are putting everything together in the basement and will try it out there, first. Everything has to be done with great care. Ben Keegan is going to be a hard man to kill."

~ Ben ~

Secretly provisioning the sailboat was a challenge, but not one that he couldn't mount. He had ordered the sailboat out of storage and once it was launched into the water, he checked all of the systems and started the diesel engine. It purred and chugged to life. Elvis, Ben's personal mechanic, had just gone over every inch of the engine room, and was wiping his hands on a rag, "Everything's in order, Chief."

After the sun was down for an hour, the two men guided the 40-foot Hinckley sailing sloop from the yacht club to the mooring in front of Clearwater Farm. It was love at first touch for Ben, as he stood at the helm. His hands grasped the leather-wrapped stainless steel wheel, sensing the weight of the keel beneath him. This sloop was designed to sit in the water and sail, but it was a piece of art as well as a well-designed yacht. He spent a few minutes examining every tiny detail in the cockpit with only the interior running lights on. The sails were pristine. He couldn't wait to really take this thing for a ride.

While the boat was moored a few hundred feet away from the dock, Ben and Elvis took care as they slid the dinghy into the water and paddled soundlessly from the dock. Later that night, with snipers at their posts, Ben donned his wet suit and slipped beneath the water with provisions for the sailboat. Night after night, he swam by the light of the stars and moon, placing items into the cockpit with careful stealth. It also gave him a chance to observe the farm from the water. With the G's, he could detect any movement. They provided the best high resolution night vision he had ever experienced. One night, he saw someone move, but quickly realized it was his own man. Over the course of a week, the boat had the things necessary to sustain them for a few days, possibly longer.

The next phase of the operation would take place the last weekend in May. It was the day prior to Memorial Day. The set-up was in progress. In a few more days, they'd start setting up the picnic on the beach. The furnishings were assembled and piece by piece items were placed gradually, to create the setting they wanted. The only unknown was: how many uninvited guests would arrive at this party? There were many eyes and ears watching and listening to his plans. He had an open communication channel going, allowing Saleh to tape record the phone calls. As actors, each played his part, although Ben continually felt a sense of dread regarding the uncertainty.

Tossing and turning at night in bed, Lara would soothe him. This was the closest he had been to bringing her on a mission. Except, this time, the mission was brought to his doorstep. He was amazed that he could function at all, but pleasantly surprised that she managed to divert his attention just long enough to stop the horrible thoughts that invaded his mind every night.

Sexual romps with her became his tension reliever. He suspected it was the same for her, too. Often, they'd shower together and make love in the morning with the hot water pulsing over them. Whenever they did, it reminded him of St. John and the first time he made love to her, only a year ago. Now that moment seemed to be in the distant past.

Occasionally, she would pull him into the master bedroom in the middle of the day and start removing his clothing hurriedly, as if she couldn't wait to have him. She seemed to know what he needed before he did. She put a deadbolt on the bedroom door, and for an hour she could take him to a place that was heavenly. Once she whispered to him, "If I'm going to die, I want to be in your arms, kissing you, loving you. When I get lost like this, I forget what is taking place out there. I need you, Ben." His heart melted when she said things like that. He felt so lucky to have her for his wife. The tension of all that was happening only served to bring them closer, which was what he hoped for all along.

As he pulled off the wetsuit in the quiet pre-dawn hours in the mud-room, he padded softly toward the master bedroom and slipped back into bed. He thought Lara was sleeping, but when she rolled over to face him, her sensual kiss surprised him. Her hand moved over the back of his neck as she kissed him like he had never been kissed before. Whenever she brought her lips to his, it activated something in him, primal and raw. Velvety and full, her lips were on his and he was overwhelmed with the love he felt for her at that moment.

When she pulled away and moved atop him, he perceived an eagerness in her eyes. With hair askew, she held his gaze for a long moment and he felt a potent energy rush through him. Her glance was seductive, filled with longing. His eyes dropped slowly to her shoulders, then to her erect nipples; he felt something instinctive stir within him. With one hand he pulled her closer, putting his mouth over her breast, gently touching her nipple with his lips. Her breathing became shallow, irregular and he felt her becoming stimulated as her dark hair fell over him. This was the response he wanted to provoke. Immersed in pleasure, he heard her make a delightful sound that spurred him on.

~ Lara ~

Ben's lips on her body made her quiver, and she knew in a moment she'd be losing control, but it was what she wanted right now at this moment. As he suckled her nipples, she felt his hands slide down past the curve of her lower back to her bottom. Instinctively, as he cupped her bottom with his hands, she moved her hips back and forth over the hardness she felt between her thighs. There was no stopping as waves of pleasure engulfed her. She was riding his erection and losing control. She pulsated and tingled with pleasure for a moment, then tumbled down upon him, breathing irregularly in his ear.

"I'm sorry, Ben. I couldn't stop myself..." she exhaled.

"Don't *ever* be sorry. I love that...so much, you will never know." Ben smiled. His dimples were showing. A hint of mischief sparkled in his blue eyes. "You have no idea how much you make me want you, when you move....like that."

He took her hand and guided it to the place she had just straddled. As her hand moved over his hardness, she felt an insatiable desire to caress him. She smiled as his hands brushed her hair away from her face and his mouth was on hers, tongue probing the seam of her lips. She gently sucked on his bottom lip and felt him inhale sharply, as her hand moved over his hardness. "I want you." She whispered.

She watched his eyes close and she took her cue to move lower, covering his chest and abdomen with wet kisses along the way. Her hands were both on him as she looked at his handsome face in the dim light. He was observing her every movement, every touch, every kiss, immersed in a state of full arousal. Her fingers tightened around his straining erection and her lips lightly encircled the swollen masterpiece. As she continued with a slow and steady motion, she could hear him making a sexy sound, one of pleasure, she knew. Stroking and sweeping her tongue over and over, she felt him growing. His body tensed and she moved her mouth away to watch the glorious reaction. A sensual volcano erupted before her eyes. She was mesmerized watching him explode with pure gratification. Strong desire coursed through her as she viewed his pleasure on full display.

After a few moments, he pulled her to him and kissed her tenderly. She loved this moment the most, when Ben was spent, totally relaxed, and he held her in his strong arms. She felt his hot breath in her ear. "I want you again, you know…" she could feel his smile against her face.

"Yes. I want you, too," she whispered back. That morning was one she would remember forever. A perfect morning tucked away to dream about when Ben wasn't there. Lovemaking with Ben was always filled with surprises mixed with tenderness. She couldn't imagine life without him, without this connection, their hearts beating together. Although the carnal pleasures were intoxicating, she was in love with the man inside. That's what made her heart rate quicken, Ben, as a man -- and all of the qualities that made him who he was.

~ Abdul ~

Tonight would be the big moment Abdul had been waiting for. Even though the celebration Keegan had been planning was supposedly kept under wraps, Abdul's men had reported back to him hourly about the movements at Clearwater Farm. It was a warm spring day, a Sunday, the infidels' sacred day. The day before Memorial Day. Good. Let them enjoy their memorial for the dead. Soon, they'd be among them. And, Abdul would secure the half million bounty and the coveted place next to his father, second in command.

Saleh had proven himself to be a good foot soldier. His information was constant and detailed. Perhaps he had gauged him wrong after all. Ibrahim was bringing ten more Americans from the cell in Massachusetts. They were not familiar with the Clearwater Farm layout, but he was showing them what needed to be done. They would be good to use as an offensive line. If they got killed, it was no big deal. They could shout Allah Akbar and go to hell for all he cared. They were expendable, and in the scheme of things, would be used to draw the enemy's fire. Abdul knew he was walking into a dangerous situation. He didn't trust the devious Navy SEALs. But, he knew how they worked. He'd have to find them in order to shoot them.

Khouri had proven to be a wildcard, just as he'd expected. Not knowing how to stifle his urges, Abdul tried to keep a tight rein on him, but Khouri was out at night drinking alcohol, picking up women in bars and fornicating. He knew this was against the teachings of the Quran, but he did it anyway. Khouri was a hypocrite, but then so was he, on occasion.

Abdul had bedded a young American girl in her teens just a few nights ago. Khouri brought her to the apartment and she was drunk. She was fourteen, so she said, and he knew that she was old enough to supply him with what he needed – a release from all of this pent up tension and aggression. She cried when he experienced his lustful urges, but then all women seemed to cry. They didn't understand him. The American women were arrogant. Didn't they know they were supposed to be subservient? That was one of the reasons he so hated American women. They thought too highly of themselves and often lived without a man. Although he was aroused when he watched them gyrate on pornographic websites, he was disgusted with them in the same vein. He wanted women, yet he felt a self-loathing, at times so strongly, he could not tolerate it.

Islam was an all or nothing proposition. Abdul knew little else except for what his father had taught him and what he learned in school. As a young child, he was taken from his mother and put into a Madrassa, taught Wahhabism, and was often beaten for not following every rule. He knew he was not living by the tenets of the ideology he was taught, but then wasn't it all a matter of interpretation? He was taught to be deceptive in order to serve Allah. So, deception was how he lived his life.

The Quran sat on his bedtable as he had sex with the fourteen year old American girl. He had glanced at it with no feeling, as he performed what was his duty as a man. He practiced the rules and regulations that suited him. Most often Abdul thought of how proud his father would be if he died in the line of duty killing the infidels. Would his father love him then? But, after thinking about being a martyr, ending it all, not having sex, not enjoying life, he would pull back from those thoughts. It was his father who needed to be killed. Then, he, Abdul, could take his position of power. He knew what he had to do.

The killing of Keegan had to come first to garner the respect he so deserved. Then, his father's superiority would be over. The will he exercised over Abdul and Ibrahim would be finished. Abdul would take him down. His father would no longer rule. It was his destiny.

~ Saleh ~

"Everything seems to be in order." Saleh said as he walked in on Abdul, but he seemed to be having a daydream. As Saleh glanced at Abdul's computer, he noticed how he quickly minimized the screen. Saleh imagined he was on a porn site again. For someone so staunch with his words, Saleh realized the pompous hypocrite Abdul really was.

Abdul finally spoke. "Ah, that is good. Sit down. I want to talk about the hit." Abdul kicked a chair toward him and zipped his fly. Saleh averted his eyes. He was always nervous about what Abdul was going to ask him. Saleh kept his anxiety hidden. Abdul had dark circles beneath his eyes as if he hadn't slept for weeks. He did not look well.

"So, you have just come from Keegan's place?" Abdul grunted. "What's the number in his army? Has he brought more soldiers to help him?"

"No." Saleh responded. "In fact, I think they are relaxed and going outside more every day. They are becoming comfortable. I think they might even be under the assumption that we have gone. They seem to be feeling a sense of security. The time is right to strike."

Abdul didn't like Saleh telling him what to do. "What makes you think this is the right time?" he asked pointedly, his dark eyes flashing, roaming over Saleh making the anxiety worse. Perspiration ran down his back, but Saleh did not waver. In fact, he met Abdul's eyes with defiance.

"It's just a feeling I have. From watching them, they are acting more normal. They are not as guarded. By leaving them alone and just watching, as you ordered – it has worked. It's a good thing Khouri did not get loose and crazy. He would have tipped them off and made them go into hiding again. They'll never be easy targets if they're hiding."

Abdul ran his hand over his beard. Saleh was correct. It was *his* plan that created this unguarded moment. Perhaps Saleh was much smarter than Ibrahim or any of the others.

"Tonight, then." Abdul leaned toward him, causing Saleh to almost stop breathing. For the past few months, he realized Abdul was as crazy as his father and he needed to be put down like the rabid dog that he was.

The others filtered in, there were fourteen in all. Saleh watched as Abdul fist-bumped Ibrahim and hugged his brother. Then Tim and Khouri arrived. Lastly, the other ten from Massachusetts rolled in. They'd been smoking at a hookah bar in town and reeked of whatever it was they smoked. Abdul went over the details one last time. The sun was setting, they were ready to strike. The cache of weapons in the dining room was handed out. Body armor was adjusted and night vision goggles were tucked into their sacks. They had obtained six rented BMW's. In the dusk, they quietly loaded the grenade launcher and AR's into the trunk along with plenty of ammo. Gasoline and other incendiary devices were careful put into the backseat area with the window rolled down.

As Saleh got into the backseat, the gasoline fumes were pungent. He slipped the keffiyeh over his head. The black scarf would act as a face cover in the darkness and would also serve to hide their identity if security cameras captured them. Saleh glanced at the night sky, a full moon tonight. It was cloudy but the air was still, as if waiting for something to happen.

Saleh had kept the men busy at the hookah bar and knew for a fact that Ibrahim and Khouri had been upstairs with prostitutes most of the afternoon. Tim spent time getting the newcomers up to speed. Abdul had been under the assumption the group had been scouting Keegan's movements, when – in fact – none of them had been watching Keegan.

Saleh knew exactly what he had to do. He had played the actions out in his mind a hundred times. First you must become the monster to hunt the monster. The drive to Clearwater Farm was a short one. They found a wooded area to hide their vehicles. He estimated they were about a half mile out. As they approached the bluff that looked over Keegan's residence, loud music was playing – it sounded like country music. The pungent smell of burning seaweed and pine boughs drifted toward them, the prevailing wind was coming off the water. Saleh could hear men laughing as they approached. Running silently though a wooded area not covered by Keegan's security camera, they got as close as they could without tripping the alarm.

"Spread out." Abdul whispered and motioned. The ten new guys moved to the east and west creating a perimeter. Saleh volunteered to carry the RPG, knowing full well it wasn't loaded with a real rocket. He hoped to God that Keegan's men would kill them before they figured him out. Abdul walked behind him with an AR15 pointed directly at him, motioning for him to continue.

Fort Gorges

~ Lara ~

"Oh God, this is primitive." Monique glanced at Lara in the darkness of the ancient fort. The women and children were camping there in silence.

"We need to do everything exactly as Ben explained." Lara was focused on the details. "You and I need to stand guard. The important thing is to keep the children quiet. They will sleep now from the sheer exhaustion of today. That's the one good thing about doing this at night."

Covered with moss and vines, the granite fort was an amazing hiding place. There were plenty of mice scurrying around her feet, nosing their way toward their provisions. Or, were they rats? She wasn't sure, but the lantern kept them away for the most part. Occasionally, she'd pick up a stone and toss it quickly toward one. She didn't want to call too much attention to them. The vermin would be back in their sleeping holes by daybreak.

She shivered, wondering what was happening on shore, but realized it was up to her to make sure Monique was up to the task of killing someone, if it came down to that.

"Here's your ammo. I've laid it out in piles for you. This is the perfect place to see anyone approaching. This opening in the fort was an old gun turret. It was designed to give you a perfect view while remaining protected." Lara explained nervously. "Let's get the body armor on. It's important."

The two women solemnly snugged their body armor on and wore helmets with G's. When looking through the G's, Lara could see everything just as if it was broad daylight. It also served as a com device, and she could see the positions of Ben's men all around Clearwater Farm. He'd left explicit instructions not to contact him or the team unless it was an emergency. Their coms were on listen only mode. The two women could hear the team's communiques to one another.

"This is amazing." Monique muttered as she listened to the men speaking to each another in one-word sentences. "They're surrounding the guys who think they're surrounding them...I can hear every voice and know who they are. This must be what it's like to be on a battlefield. It's fascinating."

"No matter what we hear, we need to stay safe and protect this group. That's what Ben explained. He said it could get very bad. We cannot assume anything until he gives the all clear signal. We need to follow his orders, no matter what."

Monique nodded, but Lara knew she was listening to the sounds of the Dark Horse Guardians as they hid in blinds and climbed trees. There would be no sleep on this quiet balmy late May evening. Just watching, listening, waiting – and praying for the best. She kept one eye on the rats scuttling nearby, and one eye on her watch post in the turret forty-five degrees away from Monique's. The thought crossed her mind that someday, she'd look back on all of this and marvel at how she did it. She imagined sitting on the beach of Clearwater Farm with Ben, kissing him, holding his hand, happy again. Relaxed.

But, the little cynical little voice that lived in the back of her mind invaded her happy imaginary scene. *You fool. What did you think would happen when you married a black-op? This is your life. Get used to it.*

Chapter 15

~ Ben ~

With the sophisticated G's, the team communicated with minimal sound. The hunting blinds built little by little, night after night, were now their hiding spots. He had gone over the details in several well-planned tactical sessions. They'd take no prisoners this time.

The snap of a dried twig alerted Ben and Elvis in the cover of the blind. With the G's, they could see the position of each man approaching. Ben was hindered by the wound in his shoulder. Everything took longer. His muscle was shredded by the bullet he took and still healing; he only hoped this would not alter his shooting skills. He controlled his breathing as he watched each man stationed around him. Slowly, their targets made their way and he watched their movement as if it was broad daylight. He had played this out so many times, the scope and layout of the battle before him was familiar.

He knew once the first shot was fired, it would be a blood bath. Most imperative was the safety and survival of his men. If every Dark Horse Guardian survived, it would be a successful mission. That was all he cared about at the moment. He waited until the targets walked past him, a good distance away, before he let out a long, slow breath and whispered, "Now."

Simultaneously, the gunfire was deafening. Silver shadows pumping ammo into bodies, with the precision of the perfect hunting party. The lasers painted their targets before they even knew what was happening. But as each body dropped, they popped off rounds in a cataclysmic cacophony. Ben knew he hit three of the targets center mass.

As the ten minutes of complete chaos subsided, he spoke into the G. "Hey, check-in time...." With his heart pounding, he waited and listened. Elvis, Gus, Tom, Nate, Rusty, Bettencourt, and finally the detectives all said their names. The back-up team, comprised of Navy SEALs, Marines and Rangers each spoke. Gus got hit with a round in his leg, but he had pressure on it and said it didn't hit the artery. Rusty twisted his ankle, but said he'd be all right.

"Okay. Stay put. I want to make sure these guys are dead. Elvis and I will be walking out there, so hold your fire. We've got our HK's. Stand by." Ben ordered.

Elvis moved silently with Ben. The two had their backs at a forty-five degree angle and rotated wordlessly as they'd done a million times on the battlefield. Stepping over the first body, Ben immediately recognized Abdul. He had been the last in. What a leader. Ben pushed his body over with his foot. "One less piece of shit on this earth." He murmured.

As they moved further, in the foreground, a figure moved on the ground, and Ben heard the voice of Saleh. "Help me..."

"Let me take care of him..." Ben ordered Elvis to step back. Bending down, he pulled the keffiyeh off the young man's face. Saleh was in pain. Ben took his weapon and unloaded it, then set it aside. Rendering aid to Saleh, he noticed his wound was painful but not fatal. He was shot in the hip, but a major blood vessel had not been severed. Ben wrapped the keffiyeh around the wound to slow the bleeding.

"This damned thing is good for something." Ben said as he touched Saleh's hand. "Stay here. The medics are on their way and will treat you. I've tagged you as a friendly."

The deal with Saleh had been simple: *give me these guys and I'll take out your father. Then, you can become the ruler of the Islamic power base and I'll support you.* Pain sometimes created incredible strength and determination. Ben learned that Saleh had personally suffered at the hands of the evil bastards running the sociopolitical show. Raped at the age of nine by a group of tribal leaders, *Saleh longed for a different ideology.* He felt compelled to do this thing, said it was his destiny. And, Ben agreed to help him, with no one knowing. Letting Saleh take the credit would make him a popular leader. And, Ben knew: *This would be how change was made, from the inside out.* Giving good men, like Saleh, a power base, bestowing rights upon women, treating children with kindness, teaching them civility and a deep reverence for life. *But, first Saleh had to survive this night.*

Little by little, with the help of Elvis, Ben walked by each body, photographing each face. Once fourteen were accounted for, Ben spoke into the com. "The detectives can call the police. We have one here alive. He's the friendly. Need a bus for him. Meat wagon for the rest."

Now that the worst was over, he checked in with Lara. "You okay, darlin?"

"Yes, we're fine. What happened over there? I watched it play out in real time, but did I hear Rusty and Gus say they were hurt?"

"Minor stuff. Not to worry. We've got the local boys coming to clean up the aftermath. Will be out to get you in a few minutes. Hang tight."

The next hour was filled with detectives and ballistic experts. The team congregated on the beach momentarily, with the android dummies that were their saviors. Gus was being treated for his wound. Rusty's ankle was wrapped securely. Ben's shoulder wound had opened up again and was bleeding. The medic bathed him with antiseptic and sewed a few stitches. His adrenaline took care of the pain for the moment.

"Damn. We did it." Ben felt giddy for a moment as he looked at the robots. "Dark Horse Guardians ~ they look like dummies, but they're not." The sound of the team's laughter drifted over the water. His thoughts turned to Lara and Monique...the women and children. "We've got to get the fort."

It seemed to be a routine thing, pushing the rigid inflatables into the water, hopping in and starting the motors. Pulling up to the side of the forty-foot sailboat, Ben started the diesel engine and pointed the sloop in the direction of Fort Gorges.

It was actually a quick trip, from Clearwater Farm to the fort...usually took about twenty minutes. Moonlight illuminated the faces of the Dark Horse team in the inflatable following him as they crossed the small stretch of ocean to the fort. He imagined Lara would be happy to hear the news that everyone was accounted for, even though there were minor injuries. But as he approached the one and only spot to get onto the island safely, he noticed a skiff tied up. It was drifting. It didn't look familiar. The moment he saw it, a strange feeling came over him. Hackles.

He shut off the diesel engine and let the sailboat glide up to the mooring ball. With one swift movement, he hooked the line in the water and secured it to the stainless cleat on the boat. With his wetsuit on, he slipped beneath the surface of the water and entered the old fort a hundred feet from where he'd normally approach. Pulling his body out of the water, he slipped out of the wetsuit and pulled out his H&K M23 pistol and held it at his side.

Fort Gorges

~ Lara ~

Everything played out on the G's in high definition night vision. She heard every shot, listened to every man speak, and waited with bated breath as Ben searched the dead. It was nearly an hour before her cell phone chimed the second time. "Darlin, I'm sorry. It was a little crazy here for a while. Are you all right?"

"Yes," she exhaled. "Everything is fine. Except these rats are getting to me. When can you bring us back?"

"Right away. We're on our way with the boat. And, darlin, I love you. You did a great job." She heard him whisper. The phone call ended and she began packing the ammo and guns away. The children were sleeping. She let the other women know the danger had passed. They would be going home. They hugged one another silently, some weeping. A feeling of tremendous relief passed through Lara.

Standing with her arm around Monique's shoulders, she glanced at her friend. "You really stepped up to the plate, Monique. I'm glad I have you as a BFF."

Monique smiled. This time she looked like the old relaxed Monique. "Thanks, I couldn't have done it without your encouragement."

"We helped one another." Lara whispered. The ocean air felt damp and cool. Both women stood in silence as the waves lapped at the shore. "Ben will be here soon with the sailboat. He'll get us all back ashore in short order."

Thirty minutes later, she could see the running lights of the sailboat. The outline of Ben's figure moving over the deck as he moored it safely off the dangerous ledge, then he dropped his body into the water and she lost sight of him. Minutes passed, that seemed to stretch into hours. She listened to her heart pounding in her ears. As soon as she saw Ben step upon the pebbly beach, his eyes met hers. Lara ran to him, embracing Ben as if he'd been gone for months. She couldn't help the tears of relief that welled in her eyes. "Oh, Ben, I was so worried…"

She heard a loud crack. The undeniable sound of gunfire. Turning toward the sound, Ben reached for his weapon. "Get into the fort, quickly, zig zag….move!" Lara watched from the fort as Ben took cover behind a huge piece of granite. She looked at Monique. "Get the guns. It's not over yet. Someone just fired at Ben out here!"

Fort Gorges

~ Ben ~

All bets were off. Ben was now playing a deadly game of tag with someone he couldn't see or hear. Without the G's, he was using only his senses. He reached for his phone in the waterproof envelope on his holster. His mind raced a hundred miles an hour as he dialed Elvis. "Hey, there's someone popping off rounds at me out here at the fort. Jesus, who the hell is it?"

Elvis replied. "We're almost there. We're just behind the sailboat in the inflatable. Hang on."

Ben breathed into the phone. "Do you have the G's? I'm blind here. Don't know where this guy is."

He heard Elvis' reply, "Yup," and the phone call ended.

More rounds were fired. It was a large caliber rifle and the last shot just grazed the fort above him. He moved inside a granite encasement, with a small opening. It felt like he was in a cave with an opening above. Good in some ways, but no exit point. Damn. This could be a death trap. Texting Lara, he told her to get the Silver Shadows and take position at the casements, being careful to remain as hidden as possible behind the granite.

Another bullet struck the hard stone surrounding him. He was the target, no doubt. But now he had brought the danger right where he didn't want it to be. And he was putting the women and children at risk, exactly what he didn't want to do.

Damn! He'd counted fourteen bodies. *That was what Saleh told him.* He had depended on Saleh to tell him the truth. Maybe that was a big mistake. Trusting Saleh could become his undoing. *Focus.* He had to find out where the shooter was set up. With a rifle, he had to have a flat spot. He studied the topography of the island on his phone again. From where he was sitting, there were only two possible places.

Like an idiot, he had taken his body armor off and he was shirtless. He took the dirt and smudged his face and chest to conceal himself, but realized it didn't make much difference. This shooter had drawn a bead on him and if he emerged, smudged or not, he'd be dead. Angling himself in a prone position, he knew the range of the MK23 was significant. Dependent upon his hearing and vision, he got eyes on the one position he thought the rounds came from, maybe he could get a well-placed shot off. Ben detected movement. A well-concealed figure moved ever so slightly and Ben fired, getting off eight rounds before pulling back against the granite.

Another burst of bullets peppered the granite that surrounded him, ricocheting all over the damned place. He called Lara on the phone. "Stay away from the openings. I know where he's shooting from, but I can't get to him. Bullets are flying all over here." Ben heard the children crying and the muffled sounds of mothers comforting them.

"Give me the shooter's position." Lara said.

"About twenty yards southeast of your turret. Maybe a bit more distance than that. Damn, I'm sorry. I couldn't be in a worse position. Stay covered and be ready to shoot if I get hit."

He called Bettencourt. "I know where the shooter is, I'm sending you the coordinates right now. Jesus, be careful. He's got a high caliber AR and he's a good shot. I'm pinned behind a huge piece of granite, well covered. I'll give you my exact position."

Within minutes there was a suppressed burst of firepower, different than the sound of the AR. Ben instantly recognized the Silver Shadow's muffled sound, then heard a body drop onto the ground less than a hundred feet from him.

He heard Lara's excited voice, "Did I get him?"

Ben watched the figure on the ground for a few seconds. No movement. "Hold on. Hold your fire." He walked toward the body on the ground and used his foot to secure the weapon. Still no movement. Blood was pooling around the lifeless man, creating a grotesque scene in the moonlight. She'd hit him center mass. When he pulled out his iPhone and searched through the photos, he used his phone to illuminate the face of the dead man. He had a match.

He instantly called Bettencourt. "He's dead. Lara killed the shooter. It was that Khouri bastard. The guy we had almost no intel on." Within ten minutes, Bettencourt, Tom, and Rusty scrambled ashore to where Ben was standing. "Thanks, guys. Good response time. But, Lara beat you to it."

Lara emerged from the fort, and Ben ran to her. "Good shot, darlin." He couldn't stop the pride swelling in his heart or the stream of tears that ran down his face for that moment. It was dark. No one would see him crying. He was just so damned proud of her. He never imagined she'd have the fortitude to save his life, but she did. The woman he held in his arms was filled with courage, grit and determination. Never did he feel so fortunate to draw a breath.

In the aftermath, he could not stop thinking, what if he'd been killed right there? There were so many things he hadn't said to Lara. So many experiences he wanted to share with her. He wanted more time on this earth, and knew he nearly got killed more than once during the past few months. Now she was part of his black-op life.

As he released her, Ben stepped back and watched as the team surrounded her, slapping Lara on the back. They all shook her hand. "Damn fine." Tom said. Ben watched as Rusty tenderly embraced her. "Just how we taught her, right Ben?"

Almost unable to speak, Ben felt the words emerging, "Yup, exactly. Let's get the hell out of here." He tried to focus on getting the women and children into the inflatable and onto the sailboat. They were going home. It was over, for now.

~ Lara ~

Something shifted inside of her the night she killed Khouri. There weren't words to describe the feeling she had when she pulled the trigger. It wasn't elation or excitement, but a sense of satisfaction. The same feeling she had when she hit the moving targets' center mass when practicing. Not the heart-racing adrenaline rush she felt when she killed the first time. *But something changed.* She had saved her husband's life. Privately, Ben showered her with compliments, knowing she didn't enjoy being the center of attention, even for something as positive as killing a badass terrorist.

"You're ready..." he whispered to her later that night, when they were alone.

"I know." She nodded. When she looked into his blue eyes, there was an understanding so powerful, she couldn't describe it with words. Lara knew the obligation that came with becoming a black-op with Ben. It was an all or nothing proposition, an all-consuming way of life. But, she wanted it. She wanted him. She remembered his voice, the look in his eyes, when he spoke the words, "Think about it..."

While she was pondering Ben's proposition, day-to-day life for them had changed dramatically. News coverage was relentless. Lara hid behind the security guards at the bungalow when working with Monique on design plans. Ben was pestered at the university non-stop. Finally, the university made a statement to the press. But, nothing seemed to stop the thirst the media had for Ben and Lara's brush with death. *Terrorists, on American soil.* It was the hot news story of the month, and they were the centerpiece of the mania. But, she knew, eventually, another news event would come along and take the place of this one. Oh God, it just couldn't happen fast enough for her.

The next month became a blur. The Dark Horse Guardians had moved back to their respective communities and kept a low profile, while Lara struggled to maintain a normal schedule. She hadn't been prepared, mentally, for the aftermath of the shooting. The press chasing her, hounding her, was more frightening than the actual shooting, itself. Her nightmares returned. The only way to stop them was to push forward, confide in Monique. Meeting with design clients, she immersed herself into work. It helped, but at night, when she closed the windows at Clearwater Farm, the images of that horrific night were viewed in her mind's eye as a movie playing fast forward.

Killing Khouri stirred something deep and primal inside of her. It was similar to the feeling she had when she killed her attacker many years ago. A sense of satisfaction knowing she did something extremely difficult -- but for the right reason – *he didn't deserve to be among the living*. For the first time, she contemplated what it would be like to work with Ben and his team undercover on a mission. She felt a unique bond with the men. They now treated her differently, as if she'd passed some sort of test.

Ben was due home any moment. The familiar sound of the Indian motorcycle rumbled outside. It was the last day of classes at the university, meaning Ben was free for the summer. She opened the door as she watched him kick the stand under the bike.

"Hey, handsome mystery man..." she called to him. Her heart always raced when his eyes first connected with hers. She craved the warmth of his embrace, his kiss, listening to his voice. She knew it would always be this way with him, even twenty years from now. She loved everything about him, even his faults.

"How about a ride on this nice warm day, darlin?" he smiled with his whole face, eyes dancing, dimples displayed. The slight tan looked good on him, as if he needed anything to make him more handsome.

"I'd love that." She said, "Let me get my bag." Moving back inside, she tossed a few items into her backpack and returned to him. "It's like....before."

"Let's go to the roadhouse for dinner tonight. I won't keep you out too late." He held her close and nuzzled her neck. "I don't want you to get too tired."

"That would be fun. I didn't have dinner planned." She noticed a gleam in his eye. As she mounted the bike, Ben waited as she put on her helmet and goggles. He secured the strap and placed a light kiss on her lips. He waited until she wrapped her arms around his sturdy waist. With a blast of excitement, they were off. The smell of blooming flowers and fresh rain on the hot pavement moved past her. How beautiful and terrible life could be all at the same time. On the back of the motorcycle with Ben, she wished she could freeze this unspoiled moment in time.

The roadhouse was filled with people on the warm June evening. As Ben walked through the door, he was met with handshakes all around. Surprising Lara, the men and women shook her hand, too. The veterans smiled and muttered things like, "Damn fine job." It wasn't celebratory as much as a form of recognition; a nod for a job well done. She soaked it in, secretly reveling in the feeling.

When they arrived at their usual corner table, Bettencourt and Monique were there.

"Damn, fancy meeting you here!" Bettencourt stood, slapped Ben and hugged Lara. The four of them decompressed over dinner and music. Lara and Monique talked about the small day-to-day crazy things. For the first time in weeks, Lara let herself go. She laughed uncontrollably. The veterans stopped by their table and included her in their humor-filled repertoire. She felt she belonged there. A unique dynamic was taking place; the men and women she so admired were accepting her into what was, possibly, the most exclusive club in the world. She never imagined she could feel this good in a crowd of people, but, she did.

This was her place. These were her people. She never felt so at home.

Chapter 16

Central Intelligence Agency, McLean, Virginia

~ Director Ali Najjar ~

Pacing the floor before the upcoming meeting usually helped Najjar focus on what he was going to say. Walking back and forth in his office often served to help him organize his thoughts. But, today there was only one thing on his mind. *Lieutenant Ben Keegan was still alive.* He wondered how the simple removal of the man had not been accomplished. What excuses would they have? He had already heard a few of them. And, if that was all they had, there would be hell to pay. He wasn't fond of the Special Activities Director, Kip Larson, anyhow. The man was too conservative and protected Keegan way too much.

A tap on the door from his secretary signaled it was time to go into the conference room for the executive meeting. He took the laptop and walked swiftly down the hallway to the room already brimming with people. Senate Intelligence Committee members and Assistant Directors. Once everyone was assembled, a hush fell over the room.

"Let's begin." Najjar said sternly. "Khouri is dead. He was our man. What the hell happened? I want answers. The press is having a field day with this. Who's going to start?"

Kip Larson stood and walked to the front of the room, and stood next to the director. Najjar figured Larson would speak, but didn't think he'd be so bold as to move to the front of the room next to him. The audacity of this asshole. Let him hang himself in front of everyone present. It would save him a lot of time and energy.

"I'll go over the details." Larsen started, "But, before I begin, you need to know that Keegan was aware of this plan all along. Don't ask me how he knew about it, but he did. That's why he is still alive."

For the next forty minutes, Najjar listened as Larson described every move made by the terror cell to take out Keegan. It was, as he expected. Inexperience. Incompetence. Stupidity. Sloppy work.

Keegan had to be eliminated; he knew too much and was more of a liability than an asset because of it. Larson was wrapping up his sad little account of what happened, or didn't happen. Larson's job was on the line, as was Najjar's. Didn't this idiot realize that fact? The president was furious. Someone's head would roll for this. Maybe more than one. He wondered sometimes how the Agency even functioned. The bureaucracy had grown to an unwieldy machine, clogged with assistants, special assistants, and inexperienced simpletons. Kip Larson didn't tell him anything he didn't already know.

When Larson sat down, Najjar delivered one message to the room full of so-called experts.

"I'll deliver my report to the President. He will make the final decision as to who will be accountable for this inept sequence of errors. Meeting is adjourned."

Najjar left the room first, but could hear them buzzing as he walked down the hallway to his office. His recommendation would be to fire Kip Larson. The Special Activities Director had grown too close to Keegan. Plus, Najjar had someone else in mind for the position; a person who had ties to his consortium, The Muslim Fellowship Group.

"Would you like to go to Prince Edward Island for a week or so?" Ben asked Lara at the roadhouse. He watched her eyes light up with delight as she smiled. Her expression said all he needed to know.

"Yes, I'd love to." Her hazel-green eyes met his and he felt his heart melt.

"Want company? Or, just the two of us?" Ben kept his eyes locked with hers.

"Maybe just the two of us for a few days, then company?" she said softly.

The thought of the two of them alone at the remote cottage was thrilling. Just what they needed. The last time they were there was tenderly remembered as one of the best weekends of his life. He recalled every detail about it and hoped, in some way, to relive it all over again with her.

"Fly or drive?" Ben queried, watching her eyes for a reaction.

"Oh, let's drive and bring Einstein. We can stop overnight to see Alvin." Lara suggested.

"Good idea. I owe him." Ben sensed her connection to the old vet, and loved that she recognized his talents. "I'll ask Bettencourt and Monique to come up the second week...how would that be, darlin?"

"Perfect." She smiled. "A week alone, together, just us.....I miss that, Ben."

She had no idea how much *he* missed their time alone together. But any time spent with her was a bonus, and he always made the best of it.

Mild temperatures and no wind made the motorcycle ride home a sensual delight. Although he'd danced with her the past few hours, he couldn't wait to feel her hands around his chest. She moved one hand beneath his leather jacket and T-shirt until she touched the ancient coin she had given him. He felt her hand trace it, then his pecs, as he sped through the darkness with the bike roaring beneath them. Every time Lara touched him, he wanted her. The heady scent of blooming honeysuckle blew by them. Soon, strawberries would be in season. He could think of nothing but feeding them to Lara, then kissing her juicy berry-stained lips. How he missed the simple things with her when he was busy working at the university or on a mission. Tonight would be special. He'd make sure it was.

Arriving at home, he secured the helmets and goggles, and took her into his arms. "Darlin, I have missed you so much. It seems lately, all we've been doing is working, fighting off the press, trying to put things back in order."

"Then, take me inside and we will play." She said softly. He smiled as she took his hand and pulled him gently toward the door. Inside, the solitude of the house was soothing. Unable to wait another moment, he took her face into his hands and kissed her in the middle of the kitchen. Her lips tasted like the ginger ale she just finished at the roadhouse. The smell of her hair was musky and sweet; his tongue traced the seam of her full lips. She parted them slightly and a bolt of lightning shot through him.

Einstein whined and entwined his bull dog body around their legs. Lara giggled and they opened the door to let him out. Holding hands, they walked down to the water's edge. Although they were interrupted, he didn't want the mood to end. Illuminated by the moonlight, Lara's face was a vision of loveliness. His lips found hers again and now her hands were on him, lightly touching his biceps, then her hand touched the back of his neck. The feeling of her fingers entwined in his hair gave him a warm rush. His hands slid down her back and he planted them firmly on her shapely behind, as he pulled her into him. She probably had no idea how much he appreciated the curvaceous lines of her derriere.

"Let's go inside." He whispered into her ear.

Soft lamplight illuminated the bedroom, as Lara turned to face him at the foot of the bed.

"It's so quiet here....I didn't realize how much I would miss silence." She breathed the words softly. His arms pulled her to his chest.

"I can't speak, I want you so much, darlin." He nuzzled her neck, and felt her smile.

Unbuttoning Lara's shirt, his eyes dropped to her pink buds erect, waiting for his touch. He often wondered what he did to deserve her. Standing before him like this, his eyes soaked in every detail of her feminine qualities. She was a visual feast. He wanted more than ever to partake in the delights she offered to him. Kissing her firm breast kindled a desire in him that was indescribable. Whatever she wanted, he would do it. She suddenly became his Kryptonite.

He felt Lara's hands push him onto the bed. Seated now, at the foot of the bed, his arms encircled her waist and his lips were on her nipples, teasing her. He felt her breath, hot and irregular on him, which only served to ignite a stronger flame. His hands traced the feminine curve of her hips. He wanted her, but he also wanted time to stand still, as he showered her abdomen with light kisses and listened to her response.

He picked her up and laid her onto the foot of the bed. Standing above her, he saw her watching him from half-closed eyes. Her hair was a mess and she gave him a little smile, as if to say, *I want you right now.* He continued kissing her belly and heard her giggle. It was a sexy sound, and he knew he was doing something right because she was delighting in it. Moving lower, he planted long, wet kisses along her inner thighs, and the sounds she made told him he was right where she wanted him.

In the dim light of the bedroom, he got excited just moving her legs apart and touching that place that was oh so feminine and beautiful to him. Catching a glimpse as he parted her thighs, he imagined the pink folds of her delicate skin to be that of a lovely flower blossom, opening for him. For a long time he kissed her there, feeling her body writhe with pleasure, hearing her moan as she reached the peak of desire and begged him to stop for a moment.

All the while, his desire was ramped to a peak that was nearly uncontrollable. If she only knew how much he loved to pleasure her this way, she would probably be surprised. Pleasing her excited him. As she reached the peak of frenzy once again, he moved above her. Feeling her arms pulling him atop her, listening to her whisper, "I love you, Ben," over and over. The climax together was breathtakingly beautiful. This was making love, and it was all that he wanted for the rest of his life.

As he scooped her into his arms afterward, he waited for her breathing to become normal.

Nuzzling her neck just below her ear, he whispered, "I love you, darlin."

Then, he knew he had to tell her. There was one more mission with Saleh. And, one more person he needed to dispose of. As he explained why he had to do this, she placed her finger on his lips.

"I know." She whispered. "I understand. Just come back to me."

~ Ali Najjar ~

Washington D.C.

For six years, he'd held the position he had wanted since a young child, the Director of the Central Intelligence Agency. His life was one of making the right connections at the right time. Perfect planning, one might say. His report for POTUS was ready, and he was sweating bullets before the meeting in the inner sanctum of the oval office. He read the report one more time, making sure he didn't leave out any details. *Kip Larson would have to go.* He would be the scapegoat for this whole mess with Keegan. There was plenty of evidence to prove Larson and Keegan were renegades, doing things that were not authorized by the CIA or the president. At least, that would be how his report would read, and it would be the centerpiece of the case he would make.

The alarm on his phone chimed. Fifteen minutes. He had been waiting in the outer chamber for fifteen minutes. The sweat began to trickle down his back between his shoulder blades. His shirt collar felt too tight. Usually, he wasn't this nervous. Playing golf frequently with the president, he felt he could calculate his moves fairly well. He took a deep breath and tried to calm himself. It wasn't easy to cut the throat of a director beneath him, but this was the only way out for him. The press was making a circus out of the incident and a press briefing in the rose garden was planned for the afternoon. If there was one thing he was certain of, it was that the president was in a foul mood. Word trickled down to him that things were not running smoothly. Khouri was never supposed to die in this mission. He was the undercover operative selected by the Muslim Fellowship, hand-picked to take out Keegan.

The secretary's assistant approached him. "He's ready, sir." The walk down the hallway into the oval office seemed to be the longest of his life. Beads of sweat formed on his upper lip. Damn, he didn't have a handkerchief. The last thought that flitted through his mind was his wife, Linda. He didn't even know why her image was there. A former Miss Universe, she was stunningly beautiful and fifteen years younger than him. Although she professed her love for him, he knew she was with him for the money and prestige. But it was a deal he had become accustomed to, even liked.

Focus on the task at hand.....he inhaled as he strode confidently through the doorway of the oval office. "Mr. President, good to see you..."

Only one other person was in the room. Good. This would be a private meeting. The under-secretary of state, a minor player in the big game, Thomas Hornby, shook his hand, but didn't look him in the eye. Then Hornby sat on the sofa, absorbed in studying something on an electronic device.

"Ali..." the president started. "I want this meeting, for the record, to be short and to the point." Ali had known the president for many years, considered him a friend. Never would he have believed the words uttered next. "You will be relieved of your position as Director of the CIA immediately. I know this may be a shock to you, but the announcement will be made in two hours in the rose garden."

Ali sat frozen, unable to think or breathe for a few moments. It was as if he was in one of those nightmares where something is happening but you couldn't move or get away. He watched the president walk about the room. The man wasn't even looking at him; he just spoke as if this meant nothing to him. Just another day, one more decision that needed to be made. Meanwhile, Ali watched his entire life circle the drain and wondered where he would end up. Surely, he'd be appointed to an ambassadorship or some other position.

"I'm sorry, Ali." The president continued. "This is the end for you as a government employee. Your paperwork has been prepared and is ready in the outer office. Your office is being sorted and packed as we speak. Hornby will take you to the security area and you are to leave your badge, electronic devices and all other government issued items with him."

As Ali stood to leave the room with Hornby, there was no handshake, no goodbye, nothing. The president sat at his desk and started reading something on the computer screen. Ali's wife's face was in the forefront of his mind as he emptied his pockets with Hornby at the security area. He felt naked and alone, humiliated. All of this happened to him because of one man, Ben Keegan.

The security guard called the car service and he stood out front. The driver got out and opened the door of the limo. Ali slid in and listened to the door close for the last time. Soft, classical music played in the limo until it arrived at his 2.7 million dollar stone front townhouse. The driver got out and opened the door for him and he nodded to him, as he always did. The three-level townhouse comprised of 5,490 square feet cost him five thousand a month. Shaded by Crepe Myrtles, it had been home to him and his lovely wife for the last seven years. He tapped the security code and entered the wood-paneled entryway. Sunlight streamed in through the beveled glass windows.

The maid was out grocery shopping, as was her habit every day at this time. He walked through the spectacular library, remembering parties and private moments with Linda. The mill-work was stunning. There were four wood burning fireplaces completely restored to their original beauty. He would miss the high ceilings, hardwood floors, and fabulous wine cellar. But most of all he'd miss the rear terrace and the balcony above where he made love to his beautiful wife on more than one occasion. His eyes were drawn to the sign that Linda had hand-painted on an ancient piece of wood, *Welcome Home*, it said.

He was no longer Director of the Central Intelligence Agency. He had recently found out that his wife was having an affair with a handsome younger man. She would leave him, no doubt. He was washed up, finished. Didn't even get a comfortable ambassadorship. His debts were incalculable. He was ruined financially. His beautiful young wife, Linda, required --- no, demanded --- a lavish lifestyle that he could no longer provide. As he gazed into the antique mirror he realized he was an impotent, penniless old man.

He reached into the nightstand on his side of the bed and brought the Smith and Wesson revolver to his mouth, angling it upward. Pulling the trigger was his last and final act.

~ Saleh ~

He glanced at his phone and noted it was 9:00 PM, not the usual time to be released from the hospital. He was being spirited to the rear entrance with an undercover police escort. Saleh had not been prepared for all of this attention and hated it. The last few weeks had been grueling. Nursing a couple of bullet wounds in his leg, it seemed he'd have a perpetual limp. The press had been pursuing him since he arrived at the medical facility, but his identity and other details were not made public. The news story was piecemeal and undeveloped. The focus remained on the dead men and why they were in the United States. Keegan was the hero of the story -- the exact opposite of what the State Department wanted, he guessed.

But, he realized he'd have to get used to this new way of life. Smiling, fighting his way through crowds with bodyguards surrounding him. It would be something he'd be doing as long as he remained on the earth. He was about to execute the biggest terrorist on the planet, with the assistance of Ben Keegan. But Keegan wanted no accolades for the hit. The credit would be all Saleh's.

While in the hospital, Keegan slipped in once to speak with him. It was nighttime and he nearly gave Saleh a heart attack. But he remembered the few bits of information he imparted.

As Saleh slid into the bulletproof Escalade, he tapped his phone. "I'm on my way."

"Yup." The voice on the other end of the phone answered and the call ended. The phone was an unusual one. A burner, it had been programmed by Keegan himself, and had a geosynchronous satellite connection. Everything was encrypted.

The SUV swung into the nighttime traffic, then deftly wound through a few snarls to the outskirts of Portland, Maine. Now headed for a bunker beneath a shooting range on Panther Pond, Saleh finally exhaled and laid his head back upon the cushioned headrest. Within an hour, the vehicle had deposited him. The place was hidden and wooded on Panther Pond. A man named Rusty came to the gate and let him in.

"You're safe here, for the time being." Rusty smiled. Saleh watched as he locked the gate and they walked for what seemed like a half mile to a large building overlooking the pond. "Go ahead in. This is the range. Ben's waiting downstairs. Lots to talk about tonight."

Saleh made his way through the shooting range following Rusty to the far corner. A hidden door led to a staircase. He noticed Rusty bolted and locked the steel door as he turned to descend the stairs.

"Hey, Saleh." Keegan was there. He shook hands with Keegan and the three of them sat down at a table to talk. Rusty had some food for him.

"Go ahead, help yourself. We might be here a while." Rusty seemed to be a gracious, quiet man. Saleh found himself eating the salsa and chips and drinking a few bottles of water. There were sandwiches and Keegan motioned to him.

"Eat, please. You and I will be flying out of Logan Airport in the early morning." Keegan explained. "We will end up in an armor-plated SUV in Dera Ghazi Khan. Your father, he is expecting you. You contacted him, and gave him the story we discussed, right?"

With his mouth full of food, Saleh nodded. Keegan continued, "And you taped the phone call, like I asked you to. Can you play it back for me?"

Saleh tapped the phone and found the conversation. He watched as Keegan turned up the volume and listened raptly to each word. After listening, his eyes met Saleh's. "Good. You were perfect. He suspects nothing."

As he finished eating and wiping his face with a napkin, Saleh had only one question. "Why? Why are you doing this for me?" He couldn't understand how Keegan could be so kind to a stranger from another country. A potential enemy, really. It made no sense to him.

"I understand. You wonder what's in this for me..." Keegan said, and his steel blue eyes bore through him. "I want the bastard dead. It's as simple as that. No more, no less. You should be the guy running the show. You have a heart, a soul. Your father does not. He is ruthless.

Your people need you. This act we are about to commit, it's for the greater good….do you understand?"

"It is destiny." Saleh replied. "I've been born to do this. That's how I feel."

"You have such potential, Saleh, do you understand what the word potential means?" Keegan asked him.

"Yes." Saleh answered. "Filled with possibility…."

"You'll need a team of bodyguards. I can pull them together through a good friend of mine in the area. It's important that you realize, you will not be able to walk freely among people without protection. Once your father is out of the picture, you will have a bounty on your head. If they kill you, this will all be for nothing." Keegan stopped.

Saleh felt himself nodding. It wasn't an eager type of nod, but one of tacit approval. He knew what he was getting himself into. Life, as he knew it, would be changed forever. But, he was ready.

"Good. Sleep here for a few hours. I will wake you early and we will drive to Boston." Keegan touched his shoulder. "You're a brave man."

Saleh watched Keegan leave. And Rusty got him a blanket and pillow for the bed in the back.

"I hope you're okay with this, but I'm locking you in here for your own safety." Rusty said solemnly.

"I understand." Saleh responded. "Actually, I am glad you are doing this. Thank you."

The door closed and Saleh listened as the lock was set. The silence in the bunker was restful, with only the faint sound of air as it passed through the vent near the bunk. Saleh let his body sink into the bed and fell sound asleep. He had not felt this relaxed for weeks, maybe months. His sleep was without dreams. The next thing he remembered was Keegan tapping him on the shoulder saying, "Get up, we've got a plane to catch." It was 4:00 AM.

Chapter 17

~ Ben ~

The news of the CIA Director's suicide put a chill through Ben. He heard it as the broadcast streamed over the speaker in the car. Ali Najjar had been a thorn in his side since he started working for the CIA. Many times he wondered if Najjar was reining in Kip Larson. The relationship between the two men was shadowy and nearly non-existent.

Through his back-door investigation, it was as Ben suspected. It was Najjar who wanted him gone, because he knew too much. He played the conversation out in his mind, *Keegan has been successful, but.....the time has come to get someone else. He could ruin us if any of this stuff was ever made public.....*

Pulling up to a McDonald's, Ben was in disguise with a long dark wig and Yankees baseball cap. The license plate flipper was used three times during his travels. He ordered a breakfast sandwich and pulled away from the drive-through, eating as he drove. Saleh consumed his in four bites. Once finished, Ben explained the next step.

"Here's your passport. Your name is Basir Abbas. You're a soccer player from Morocco. Your bag is in the back of the car. It contains a soccer uniform and some personal items. It's a carry-on. No time to waste when we land. We have first class tickets. If you're asked any questions, act like you don't understand English and I will come to your aid. Got it?"

"Yes." Saleh replied. He seemed as cool as anyone could possibly be. Ben hoped he would always be this easy-going. It would make things a lot easier and would draw less attention.

The two of them passed through security with no problems. On the plane, Saleh asked what time they'd arrive in Pakistan. "You can sleep for a while." Ben assured him. "This is going to be a long flight."

His thoughts drifted to Lara, alone now at Clearwater Farm. He was hopeful she was enjoying the solitude for the moment. Her life had been nothing but chaos for the last five months. Once he finished off Salib Madi, he would be returning home.

Ben focused like a laser on what was to come. Salib Madi was awaiting his son's return. A celebration had been planned for Saleh. Ben loved homecomings that had lots of distracted people letting their guard down. He couldn't have planned a better scenario to have the gruesome ruler meet his demise. Ben was dressed as a Pakistani national with a passport confirming that. He wasn't getting paid for this hit, but the payment would come in due time with Saleh in charge. *Things would change.* He'd get intel for special forces that would be a goldmine, a treasure trove. *The tide would turn.* He would arm the women and work quietly in the background, instructing them how to kill the men who subjugated them. He would train them how to protect themselves and their children.

This was how real change occurred. Saleh was a reformer. He would be a symbol of the new age of Islam. But first the savage pigs that ruled with his father had to be put down. That's where he could help Saleh, support him with all of the might the United States had, strategically placed, to beat back the pure evil that now reigned. *This would be a different kind of war.* One of tactical moves and thoughtful strategy. So much depended upon this one significant shift. He would not allow himself to entertain the thought of failure.

~ Lara ~

Even though Ben had explained the mission to her, she felt an incredible sense of sadness sweep over her as he left to meet with Saleh and leave the country. Pakistan. She hated the place. It was filled with pockets of terrorists, many of them wanting to kill her husband. The reality of this cycled through her mind constantly while he was gone.

The phone call to Finn Murphy was a necessary one. He had always been her right-hand man at Stone and Associates, and one of her closest allies. When she spoke to him last week, he mentioned he had someone to take over her design business for the next year. She tapped the phone and he answered immediately.

"Hey, Lara, how are you?" Finn asked, his voice filled with genuine concern.

"I'll take you up on the offer." Lara said with no emotion. "How soon can you make the arrangements?"

Finn hesitated for a moment. "You're sure?"

"Yes," Lara whispered. "I've got this feeling that I need to do this with Ben. I love him more than anything in the world. I can't live like this – having him come and go for weeks, sometimes months, not knowing....." her voice trailed off as her throat tightened. She didn't want to cry.

"You've thought this through? " Finn seemed to be gauging her certainty.

"Yes, I'm certain."

"I'll have Betsy and a couple of designers come in and take over your projects. You can meet her at the bungalow this weekend to fill her in. Monique will remain?" Finn queried.

"Yes. And she will be a terrific help."

"All right, consider it done." Finn exhaled. "I will miss working with you...pestering you. You know that, don't you?"

"Yes. And, I will miss you, Finn, more than you know." Lara said. She meant every word of it. Hanging up the phone she felt one tear slide down her face, but she stopped feeling sorry for herself immediately. She had a task sitting before her that needed completion. She needed to focus on that now, so she could move forward in a new line of work with Ben and the Dark Horse Guardians. Making this decision had been exciting and terrifying all at the same time.

Ben had explained what would happen next. They couldn't live their lives exposed. They'd go into hiding for a period of time, then emerge with a different identity. Clearwater Farm would be sold. They would need to move from place to place for a long time, then eventually settle somewhere and make a life. Ben mentioned staying at Prince Edward Island for the summer. Then, a trip to Dublin.

A new administration was coming into the white house in the next few months. Rumor had it that Kip Larson would be promoted to the CIA Director's position. If that was the case, then Ben was going to be tapped to head up a special counter-terrorism unit on American soil. This was a new concept, one that the United States government was willing to pay handsomely for. A new form of Homeland Security, *one with teeth in it*. And, Lara knew, more than ever, she wanted to be a part of it all.

~ Saleh ~

Cleared at the Pakistani border, Ben and Saleh traveled with a small group of up-armored SUV's behind them. Saleh was no longer a soccer player. He had escaped America without a trace. The news consortium was now off his trail. This was home. Keegan, however, was garbed in black from head to toe, wearing a long beard and a keffiyeh, an Arab face scarf, designed to keep the sun and wind from the face, now the symbol of Middle-Eastern man. Saleh learned that Keegan also spoke perfect Urdu and Arabic, and several other dialects.

"Here's where we part." Keegan tapped his shoulder and the vehicle stopped. The man named Moshe was behind him in the small caravan. Keegan disappeared into the darkness of the night as he spoke into the com device he called a G, and about fifty pounds of equipment strapped to his body. Everything was black, even his skin was darkened with some sort of resin.

The driver of Saleh's vehicle continued on to his father's compound in the city of Dera Ghazi Khan. The other vehicles disappeared, taking another road well behind them now. As Saleh checked through the gated compound, he noted there were hundreds, possibly a thousand, people congregated there to greet him. Music was playing. There were dancing girls. It looked like some sort of festival. The crowd parted as Saleh's vehicle drove up to his father, waiting under a huge white tent. Brightly colored lights lit up the entire area.

Salib Madi stood to welcome his son, but did not walk toward him. It was a sign of deference for the son to walk to the father in this part of the world, and Saleh did so without hesitation. Saleh watched his father smile as he walked toward him.

"See, I told you he'd return – he's amazing – my son!" Saleh felt his father's strong embrace and he received a kiss on each cheek. A goat was sacrificed on the spot and the crowd cheered as they prepared it for the fire pit. Praise was chanted in Arabic. The crowd was enthusiastic.

Once the chants died down, Saleh reached into his bag. "For you, father." He held out the medallion, a beautiful work of art. Gold inlay with an intricate design of the crescent and star on a gold chain, fit for a king. Salib Madi held the gold chain in the air and called out to the crowd before him.

"My son has brought me a beautiful gift." Madi handed it back to Saleh and he slipped the chain over his father's neck. "Take a picture and put it on Facebook!" his father laughed. Saleh had never seen his father smile like that. It was a grin from ear to ear, and the cheering from the crowd was deafening. So much so, that his father did not notice when Saleh moved away, to the far corner of the tent and started walking toward the perimeter of the compound. Few people lingered in that area where there was no light.

Within a minute, he sent the text to Keegan. The target was painted and Saleh took the route they discussed, one that took him toward the bath facilities. As he entered the toilet area, he heard the explosion as the drone strike hit its target. The tent where his father had been standing was incinerated in one huge blast. A hellfire missile struck killing his father and all surrounding him.

When Saleh ran to the wreckage, few people were left alive. The ones that remained were dying. He walked away and a vehicle picked him up. The meeting was set-up for the next morning. Keegan had teams of people ready to descend and help him make sense of the chaos.

~ Ben ~

The deed was done. Saleh performed perfectly. Moshe picked him up and they moved toward the border in the darkness. Saleh knew what he had to do now. He had to play the biggest role of his life, and it needed to be an academy award performance. Those who remained in his father's army would turn to Saleh for guidance. For the many weeks and months to follow, a team of special ops from the United States would quietly and methodically kill every man Saleh marked.

Then, slowly, Saleh would take a group of specially trained Yazidi soldiers, allies of the United States, persecuted to the point of near extinction by the jihadist murderers. Little by little, the Yazidi group would swell to the size of a large army as Turks and others from the region who wanted the New Age of Islam to dawn. They'd be supported and supplied by the United States in a clandestine manner. Meanwhile, the drone strikes would continue, taking out the men Saleh marked. All of this had to be done without Saleh saying a word to anyone else about it. No confidante. No friends. Just business.

As Ben thought back on the celebratory moment, he imagined Saleh placing the medallion around his father's neck. The crowd was cheering. These men were so different than the soldiers he served with. The jihadists demonstrated their kills on YouTube, as if it was something to brag about. Taking a life was never something to cheer about. It was grim business for the special operators he had worked with all of his life.

But the difference was, the Islamic terrorists were egotistical maniacs. Ego was always at the center of evil. The men he'd served with were getting a job done and moved forward to the next task on the list. There were no celebrations or taking credit. No YouTube videos, chanting or bragging. Although, the liberal press in the United States would have their audience think differently. Often times, U.S. soldiers were portrayed as knuckle-dragging Neanderthals, torturing and killing for sheer pleasure. The ends justified the means.

The ends. Ben thought long and hard about the big difference there. Yes, both sides killed, but there was an all-important discussion to be had about the ends. Terrorists killed because they believed snuffing out life that was different than theirs was not only acceptable, but required. There was no respect for life, liberty, or the pursuit of happiness. Zero tolerance.

The ends for the Dark Horse Guardians were completely different. Their purpose was to eliminate evil that subjugated women and children and to kill those who refused to live peacefully, and tolerate those with beliefs different than their own. *The ends did justify the means.*

But the special operators did not high-five or fist bump their victories, nor did they display them on YouTube. What they did was for a greater good. They silently, methodically pushed forward, mission after mission, dedicating themselves to a life of protecting and defending freedom. These concepts were foreign to those who ruled with terror.

Lieutenant Ben Keegan wholeheartedly believed he was on the winning team. The fight would continue for some time to come, but in the end, he believed good would win. Freedom would trump subjugation. Good would defeat evil, at least it would if he had anything to do with it.

THE END

Note from the author: Thank you for reading this book.

If you liked it, please leave a review on Amazon for me.

Book 5 in the Dark Horse Guardian Series is currently being written.

Made in the USA
Middletown, DE
21 December 2017